W9-CSB-889

BLOODLINES

BLOODLINES

Gerald Hammond

Chivers Press   •   Thorndike Press
Bath, England   Thorndike, Maine USA

This Large Print edition is published by Chivers Press, England, and by Thorndike Press, USA.

Published in 1998 in the U.K. by arrangement with Macmillan.

Published in 1998 in the U.S. by arrangement with St. Martin's Press, Inc.

U.K. Hardcover ISBN 0–7540–3365–1 (Chivers Large Print)
U.K. Softcover ISBN 0–7540–3366–X (Camden Large Print)
U.S. Softcover ISBN 0–7862–1497–X (General Series Edition)

The text of this Large Print edition is unabridged.
Other aspects of the book may vary from the original edition.

Set in 16 pt. New Times Roman.

Printed in Great Britain on acid-free paper.

British Library Cataloguing in Publication Data available

Library of Congress Cataloging-in-Publication Data

Hammond, Gerald, 1926–
      Bloodlines / Gerald Hammond.
            p.   cm.
      ISBN 0–7862–1497–X (lg. print : sc : alk. paper)
      1. Large type books.   2. Cunningham, John (Fictitious
character)—Fiction.   3. Dog breeders—Scotland—Highlands—
Fiction.   4. Highlands (Scotland)—Fiction.   I. Title.
[PR6058.A55456B57   1998b]
823'.914—dc21   98-15547

CHAPTER ONE

It was the finest autumn that I could remember, that year when Sam was four. For once, the first frosts delayed until the equinoctial gales were past. Then the frosts came and the wind fell away so that the leaves hung on the trees, yellow and gold and orange and bronze and flaming scarlet, seeming to get brighter as the days went by and the sun still shone down, cooler but bright, on the Kingdom of Fife and other, less significant, parts of Britain. And people were telling each other that it would be a short winter for a change.

One of the first shoots of the season, on a morning that somehow managed to be both crisp and temperate, was Lord Crail's. I was invited to attend for once as a guest Gun rather than in the capacity of the picker-up—a humbler capacity but equally enjoyable, if not more so. Crail's account with the kennels had grown to mammoth proportions and although I had not been hurrying him—for he always paid up in the end—he had felt guilty enough to include me with the friends and sundry other creditors who were his guests. Thus he made sure of my goodwill while at the same time gaining the unpaid services of Beth and myself anyway to help with the picking-up—that is to say, the seeking out after each drive any birds hit but not gathered by hand, with the help of a selection of our dogs. The money saved on pickers-up would have gone to pay those in the beating line who were not Crail's friends or relations or beholden to him for something. Freddy Crail's life was, a long process of robbing Peter to pay Paul but somehow he always seemed to scramble through. He even managed to get from it a certain excitement appropriate to success at any game of skill.

Crail's shoot was not at his family home, where the land was mostly pasture and too flat to be suitable for showing good birds. Instead, he had managed to put together the sporting rights to three arable farms, twenty miles from his home but only five from ours.

As we turned in to a tarmac farm-road I was saddened to see two ladies, one of them young but the other definitely not, flaunting placards which bore the legend 'Ban this cruel sport'. Living as we do where shooting is part of the way of life, we had been largely free from the objectors who, further south, were rushing to destroy the old and valuable out of an ill-founded sense of righteousness.

In the cobbled farmyard between the old stone buildings which stood at the core of the shoot, Beth and Blossom and Horace and Jason and I were having a chat beside the car while we waited for the customary pre-shoot briefing (no low or immature birds, no ground game except foxes and feral cats and a stiff fine for a white pheasant in the bag). Beth is my wife. Jason was her personal Labrador and the others were springer spaniels. I was feeling good. The sun warmed my back and even the aftermath of my long illness was forgotten.

The first hint that the day might not be as halcyon as I was expecting came when Beth looked over my shoulder and said, 'Oh-oh! Here comes your *bête noire*.'

I knew who she meant, but I looked round anyway. Ben Garnet, lean and hawk-faced, was climbing out of a large estate car and looking, as usual, totally self-satisfied. I thought that I never seemed to see him in the same car twice. Either he dealt in them on the side or he took them as bad debts.

'Bugger it!' I said. I do not usually swear in front of Beth, if only because she looks far younger than her real age and much too young to be exposed to bad language. But Garnet's presence had driven the sunshine away.

In calling him my '*bête noire*', Beth had understated my true feelings. Perhaps it is because I am a compulsively honest person. In my simplistic way I yearn for a world in which doors can be left unlocked and people can trust one another; the thought of a world peopled by politicians and other crooks comes close to my vision of hell. What, I wondered, makes such people so special that they feel a right to help themselves at the expense of the rest of society? My choice of career might easily have

3

been the police except for the greater revulsion that dishonesty on an international scale triggered in me. Instead, I had opted for the army and had played my small part in the UN's policing role whenever dishonesty on a grander scale triggered riots or genocide.

In the real world between the two extremes I had envisaged, I can understand if not approve the thief who needs something, wants it and takes it. But Ben Garnet was a shark of a different breed and quite beyond my comprehension. He was not badly off so far as I could tell—although another man's financial status is not always easy to judge. A yacht or a Rolls may be a sign that he has money . . . or that he had money before he bought the yacht or the Rolls. Ben Garnet entertained lavishly in his converted farmhouse about four miles from Three Oaks Kennels. I had never been invited and never would be—his guests were usually councillors or businessmen who could be useful to him. There were rumours about girls and soft drugs at some of the parties from which his wife was usually absent—whether for reasons of tact or ignorance was never established. Status symbols were important to him. He had horses in a paddock although nobody had ever seen him ride.

News of his activities went the rounds as regularly as the dustcart, and these were never above board. When he bought into a firm it collapsed within the year, his partners were bankrupt but somehow Garnet was left to sell off the assets at a profit to himself. I knew for a fact that he had persuaded the heirs to sell him his present house at a bargain price before the previous owner was quite dead and that he still owed several of the workmen for the cost of the modernization.

But I had a more immediate and personal reason for my detestation of the man.

A kennels that depends for much of its income on training gun dogs—of its own breeding or those of outside clients—needs access to land holding game. One may get through the intermediate stages of training using pigeon and rabbits (which are not game and which the farmer has the right to control) or by using clever gadgets that simulate the flushing of a bird or the bolting of a rabbit. But before a dog has a real chance in field trials— the arena in which reputations are made or lost and values are established—real experience is needed on real game, more than can be given during those occasional days at picking-up which can be squeezed in between the inevitably conflicting trials dates.

Several years earlier we had acquired the sporting rights to Foleyknowe Estate, in partnership with a small game dealer and part-time keeper, and we had worked the shooting up to a standard which was modestly profitable on a commercial basis and a perfect training ground for the spaniels. Our successes in field trials had come more regularly and our prices, including those for stud service, had risen accordingly.

That spring, however, the owner had been abroad and, despite reassuring phone calls, our sporting lease had not been formally renewed. Then, during the summer, Mrs de Forgan, the owner, had been killed in a car smash in Spain.

It had seemed only respectful to wait patiently for the executor and trustee to come back to us. But in the meantime, Ben Garnet had got wind of the situation. He approached the executor direct and made an offer for the sporting rights. The executor told me later that Garnet had assured him that he was acting with our agreement, though Garnet denied it when I challenged him. But the damage was done, a new lease had been signed and we lost the use of Foleyknowe, the work we had done and all the birds which had already been released for the coming season.

Within days, Garnet had signed the sporting rights over to another of my *bêtes noires*, a commercial operator who I knew would show easy birds to visiting Guns at exorbitant prices and without paying even token respect to the habitat we had patiently nurtured. An ecological asset-stripper, in fact.

So I had good reason to dislike Ben Garnet. What particularly stuck in my craw was that for the sake of a modest profit to himself he had done us damage of ten times greater value. Yet, when we met, he acted as though he had done us a favour.

'If I'd known he was coming . . .' I began.

'You'd have baked a cake?' Beth suggested.

I spurned her attempt to lighten the atmosphere. 'I'd have baked him in a slow oven,' I said, 'or stayed a long, long way away.'

She nodded. 'I wonder what happened to him in his childhood,' she said.

'Nothing fatal, I'm sorry to say.'

'I didn't mean that.' Beth's smooth brow creased with the effort of expressing her analysis of Ben Garnet. 'He must have grown up feeling terribly insecure if he believes that his manhood would be threatened if he gave somebody a fair deal.'

'Is that really how you see him?' I asked.

'He seems to feel a compulsion to cheat even if he's the loser in the long run.'

'That much I know,' I said. 'It was the manhood bit that made me sit up.'

Beth ignored my disgression. 'The local tradesmen won't work for him any more,' she said. 'Sometimes they take him to court, looking to be paid, but they rarely win.'

'I believe he's a lawyer,' I said. 'But maybe only of the barrack room variety. Nobody seems to be sure about his true background, but he always has the angles covered.'

'Well, he doesn't do himself any good. He's having to bring plumbers over from Dundee when his heating goes wonky. It must cost him a bomb.'

We had no more time for idle chat. Lord Crail button-holed me for some more free advice about his dogs. The beaters went off in a trailer, their numbers swelled by some of Crail's younger relatives. Crail's head keeper, a former warrant officer in the Scots Guards who bullied Crail mercilessly and always seemed to draw his salary even when his employer's finances were at their lowest ebb, coughed once. The voice which had once been able to set a regiment in motion was reduced to a comparative whisper by the passage of the years, but he gave a commanding jerk of his head and the proceedings began.

In a way, I thought, Garnet and Crail were a pair, but Lord Crail was open and apologetic and somehow always cleared his debts in the end whereas Garnet possessed the nerve of the devil. While the usual introductions were being performed I gave him the remotest nod which would be consistent with politeness to my host but Garnet beamed and nodded as though I had kissed his feet. He knew that I despised him, but to him that knowledge was as water off a duck's back. I was never sure whether he deluded himself that the world was blind to his ways or whether he pretended, as part of a calculated front, to be unaware of the general resentment. The Fifer, like any other Scot, shies away from debt and expects another man's word to be his financial bond.

I drew number 2. To my relief, Garnet drew 6, which would keep him about as far from me as was possible for most of the day. He was a safe enough shot, but on one previous occasion when he and I had drawn adjoining pegs I had found him to be a greedy one, taking birds at long range which would otherwise have passed over my head.

The Guns had only a hundred yards to walk to where we were placed at pegs along a muddy track. The first drive was from a field of turnips. It would have been usual for a non-shooting wife to stand with her husband but Beth knew Lord Crail's second motive for the invitation perfectly well. In this way he gained the services of Beth and several of our dogs without payment of the customary token fee. She trotted away with Jason to the other end of the line and the ex-RSM hobbled off stiffly to take up a position behind the middle ground with his two Labradors sitting to attention beside him.

The beaters could be heard coming through a sparse wood that sprawled over the shoulder of a low hill. They emerged into the turnips. I felt the usual surge of anxiety-induced adrenalin. When shooting in company, the sound of each shot draws attention and every miss is conspicuous. A change in one's own reactions, a different batch of cartridges, a loss of confidence, any of these could induce a sequence of misses exposing the victim to derision. My shooting for months past had been of rabbits and the humble bunny is tied to two dimensions with only minor variations. A rabbit is to a curling pheasant as Karting is to Formula One.

One end of the beating line was still on the hillside and a Labrador put a cock pheasant out of a patch of golden bracken. Clocking angrily and climbing, the bird headed in my direction. Its colours blazed in the winter sunshine. All eyes were following it. My mouth was dry. At the last moment I mounted the Dickson ahead of the bird and squeezed the trigger as it came to my shoulder. The bird turned over in the air, stone dead, took several seconds to fall a hundred feet before hitting the ground with a thump.

Suddenly I was at ease.

The first frosts had killed off the insects in the turnips so that few birds came out of that field; and not all of those that got up were willing to climb like that first cock. Even so, a scattering of good birds were greeted by a satisfactory crackle of shots. By the time the beaters arrived and the whistle went for the end of the drive, there were several birds to be picked at my end of the line including a difficult runner in the set-aside behind us and a duo which had flown on into the middle distance before collapsing. The set-aside would be the next drive and was better left—the beaters would pick the runner on the way through. The others had made it to an area of gorse a hundred yards behind the pegs.

The two spaniels were working through the gorse when Lord Crail joined me, a well-grown hen pheasant dangling from his hand. (The birds were mostly hens. Crail had purchased ex-laying birds from a game farm, which was how he had come to have mature birds on the ground so early in the season.) His yellow Labrador had been handling well, I had noticed with pleasure. I had trained the dog for him myself and repaired the damage whenever Crail untrained him on the rabbits each summer. Crail was as sturdily built as his Labrador and with much the same colour of sandy hair.

'We're a bit short-handed on the picking-up side,' he said apologetically.

'We don't mind helping out,' I said. I looked on the help and the white lie as a discount for a favoured customer. We might sometimes have to wait for our money but Crail made up for it by singing our praises.

'That's good,' he said. 'My aunt will be along but she can't make it until after lunch.'

(I nodded. Lord Crail's elderly aunt and her golden retriever were a formidable team.)

'I see that Garnet isn't working his bitch today,' I remarked. The one thing that could be said for Ben Garnet was that when it came to dogs he knew what he wanted and made sure that he got it. From one of my clients he had

11

obtained a bitch, daughter of one of my breeding and already close to field-trial standard, and as far as I could discover he had actually coughed up the substantial purchase price. Unlike most such purchasers he had kept her up to the mark, working her in the field and even competing on occasions with modest success, although, true to type, he was not above a little bending of the rules.

'I saw Cleo in his car,' Crail said, 'but he tells me that she's in season. He says that he only brought her along because there's nobody at home to look after her. I only hope that her presence doesn't put the other dogs off their work. Shall I send Bosco in to help?'

'Not yet,' I said quickly. The last thing I wanted would be two dogs competing for the same bird.

'Garnet's backing a deal that involves a piece of my land,' Crail said. It was very close to another apology.

I wanted to tell him to hold a long spoon but decided that Crail should know his company. 'I understand,' I said.

'You can't stand the man.'

'That's hardly your fault.'

'True.' Crail paused. 'All right, so he's not perfect. But he quite likes you. He asked whether you'd be here and seemed pleased when I said that you would.'

Blossom emerged from the cover, a hen pheasant in her mouth still kicking. I took it from her and did the necessary while she grinned at me, obviously very pleased with herself. Her tail swished in the dried grass. I made her stay. I could hear Horace still working in the gorse. Blossom was frantic to go and join the fun but she had to learn that she was there to do my will, not her own.

There was a sudden stir in the gorse and a grunt. Moments later, Horace came out with the other hen pheasant, stone dead.

'That's the lot?' Crail asked. I said that it was. 'Let's get on,' he said. We walked back to where the other Guns were chatting. A flask was doing the rounds. The beaters had already gone on and as soon as we appeared the ex-RSM began to chivvy the guns towards the two Land Rovers which were standing by.

Sport picked up towards lunchtime. A cunning host will save his better drives for later in the day. A canny keeper may then send them over too high and fast for the average Gun. The fourth drive was spectacular, with birds in plenty crossing a valley and slanting downward towards home. Crail, I decided, must have been in funds around the previous June.

As shoot lunches go, that day's came somewhere near the middle of the spectrum—neither a soggy sandwich in a steamed-up car nor a sit-down guzzle in the Great House but a civilized buffet with a modest wine, served from trestle tables in a barn. There were straw bales to sit on while eating chicken legs and sausage rolls and pâté on crusty bread and juggling with salad. By then we had worked back to near where we had started. The beaters had gathered in the head keeper's cottage nearby, probably enjoying greater comfort but a less elevated menu.

I let the dogs loose. They knew better than to wander far or to get into mischief. They were more likely to hang about where the food was, pretending to be on the point of death from starvation.

Ben Garnet came and stood helping himself from the buffet beside me, but I took my plate and glass to the far end of the barn and lost sight of him—indeed, at one point I was vaguely aware that he was not there to be seen. His absence was positive rather than negative as warmth is more than an escape from cold.

I had finished my main course and taken some fruit, and I was sipping the last of my one glass of wine. It was a good wine. Freddy Crail had inherited his father's cellar and even when his finances were at their lowest ebb his wine never let him down. Beth and I were congratulating him on the morning's sport when the skinny figure of Garnet appeared in the barn's doorway, black against the brightness outside. 'Come and bear witness to this,' he said loudly. He glanced at me but seemed to be speaking to the company at large.

We trooped outside, curious rather than obedient. Several of the beaters had spilled out

14

of the head keeper's cottage.

Next to the Land Rovers a brace of spaniels was locked together in the classic position, bum to bum, of dogs at the culmination of coitus. I recognized Horace immediately. He was in demand at stud, having thrown a succession of successful trials dogs, so that I had seen him often enough in that act. The other was Garnet's Cleo.

My first concern was for Horace. 'Don't disturb them,' I whispered urgently. 'The male can be injured if they part suddenly.'

But the two must have been engaged in the act for some little time, because a few seconds later they parted quite gently and naturally. Horace, who was quite accustomed to an audience on these occasions, ambled away round the nearest cars, evidently looking for a comfortable resting place. Shortly he would come looking for the restorative biscuits which were his usual reward.

Garnet grabbed Cleo, lifted her urgently into the back of his car and then turned to me. 'You did that on purpose,' he said.

His anger lacked real conviction and any deed had been Horace's rather than mine. I would have ignored the accusation. Beth, however, lived in eternal fear that any undue stress would bring on a possibly fatal recurrence of the illness which had terminated my army career and no reassurance from myself or any of my doctors would allay that

15

fear. She flared up immediately in my defence.

'Why would John do a thing like that?' she demanded.

Garnet hesitated. It seemed that his thinking had not progressed so far as to suggest any motivation on my part. 'Sheer mischief,' he suggested at last.

Beth ignored that suggestion. 'Do you know how much we get for a service from Horace?' she demanded.

'No I don't,' Garnet said stiffly, 'and I don't particularly—'

'Well, yours will never be worth as much,' Beth snapped. There was a stir of amusement among the onlookers.

Garnet had not pursued his vocation, whatever one might care to call it, without developing the ability to keep his temper in the face of insults, but there was a trace of colour in his thin cheeks and a flare to his proud nostrils as he framed his reply. 'I have never tested the market,' he replied with an attempt at humour.

When Beth's blood was up she could bandy words with the best of them. 'Now that I've put the idea into your head,' she said, 'you probably will. But you'll be disappointed. Three of Horace's offspring have made champion already. Anyway, how did she get out of your car? Horace is clever but he can't work door-handles yet.'

'Somebody must have let her out,' said

16

Garnet. He tried to sound as though he knew something that was hidden from lesser mortals. Then he turned away.

Beth was angry enough to run after him but I caught her arm. 'Leave it,' I said. 'We can't be sure of anything. Anyway, he'll be sorry in the end.'

She looked up into my eyes. 'He will? You promise? Faithfully?'

'I promise,' I told her.

'Well, all right then,' she said reluctantly.

One of the guests, a tall man with prominent ears and sunken cheeks, was grinning. I knew him vaguely as the proprietor of a small garage nearby and I thought that if Crail did not owe him for some repairs he might have been invited in order to provide the second Land Rover for the day. 'I doubt you'll ever get the better of that one,' he said. 'There's not the least doubt that he meant it to happen, but you'll never prove it. He's a sleekit bugger, is Ben Garnet.' His tone was half admiring.

'You know him, then?' I looked around. For the moment, there was no longer anyone within earshot. 'You do business with him?'

He produced another grin, which sat oddly on his eccentric face. 'No more than I need to. He's a member of a small syndicate at Kiltillem and I'm the secretary—for my sins. Give him his due, he'll turn out for a working party though he keeps up his membership mostly so's he can hand out invites to his posh friends. But when it comes to paying his sub, well, it's his teeth I might be pulling.'

'I know the type,' I said.

'They're beginners compared to this lad. He has a thousand excuses and then some. He hasn't got a chequebook wi' him or he's used the last cheque in it or he's too busy at the moment or can I take a credit card? I can just see me carrying an Access machine on a working party! Last year he turned up at the first shoot with his sub still unpaid and no chequebook again though he'd been warned.' The watery eyes held a sudden twinkle. 'I took him aside and telled him he and his guest—he had a guest wi'm, would you believe?—would be welcome to walk wi' us, but if either of 'em fired a single shot he'd be prosecuted as a poacher. I thought for a wee minute he was going to call my bluff, but instead he pulled out a roll of notes that would've choked an elephant and settled up on the spot and carried on with the day as though nothing had happened. I dare say it'll be the same this year.'

I shook my head in disapproval. 'I couldn't be doing with that,' I said.

He shrugged. 'I made him pay cash for his petrol so now he's taken his custom elsewhere, the Lord be thankit. To be fair, he's no less friendly now than he was afore. It's as though such goings-on are normal to him. Some of the other syndicate members wanted to put him out, but his money's as good as the next man's

18

when you can get your hands on it. Also, we're a bittie short of dogs and he has the only good spaniel among the lot of us.'

'Now there,' I said, perking up, 'I might be able to help you. We've a good litter in the offing.'

'I'll mention it around,' he said, 'but don't hold your breath. At your prices . . .

'A trained dog costs money,' I admitted, 'but by the time I've fed them and had them vaccinated and inoculated and put in all the time that's needed—'

'I ken a' that fine,' he said, laughing. 'But it's no damn use being told a Rolls is good value for money if you don't have the bawbees to buy it.'

'Come on,' I said. 'You ask five times as much for a second-hand car that'll wear out or rust away in another five years. The dog'll give you ten years of faithful, loving service. There's no comparison.'

'You're right there,' he said. 'There's no comparison.'

'A pup would come a lot cheaper,' I pointed out. 'That's what I was suggesting. Your members could buy a pup each to train for themselves and come to my Masterclass, one Sunday a month. Or if there's enough of you, I'll lay on a special training class, just for you.'

A stocky figure with cropped ginger hair had arrived and had been hopping from foot to foot in front of us for the last few minutes. He was the under keeper, a youth usually referred to as Guffy. Ex-RSM Fergusson had been a strong man in his day, but the years and foreign climates had taken their toll and Guffy, who was shared between the farm and the shoot, was there to relieve Mr Fergusson of physical labour and to operate some of the farm's machinery between times. I had seen him around. He was sturdy, capable and, considering his background, well spoken although liable to lapse into the Scots tongue when upset, but outside of his limited areas of capability he was sometimes on a wavelength all his own. Though I guessed that some government body was funding some or all of his wages, I knew that Mr Fergusson would be hard put to it to manage without him. A relationship between the two was hinted at but never confirmed.

For all his slow wits, Guffy was a good shot, successful at the clay pigeons and useful at controlling vermin.

'Mister,' he said, 'how much do you take for a pup, then? A good one?'

The garageman chuckled until his eyes filled with tears. 'You should be in my game,' he told me. 'You're a better salesman than I am.'

Guffy's question put me on the spot. The boy had a knack with animals but his mental circuits were incomplete and there was no doubt that he could be heavy-handed at times. I was in the business of bringing dogs into the world but not to cast them adrift to be mishandled. Sometimes we lost business because I was overly fussy about the good intentions of prospective clients, although Beth and Isobel were solidly with me. I had made up my mind that no puppy of mine would fall into Guffy's hands.

I told Guffy the range of prices, depending on the breeding of the pups and the successes of the breeding line; but I gave him a strong hint that our puppies were all earmarked for several years ahead.

His face fell and then he cheered up. He was a naturally happy boy. 'Maybe Mr Garnet'll be looking for a good home for a pup,' he said. 'They'll be braw pups, those.'

'You have a care,' the garageman said. 'He may be looking for a good home but he'll care more about the price he gets than about how good the home is.'

'And read anything before you sign it,' Beth added, 'in case it says something about a pound of flesh.'

Guffy looked confused. 'What are you at?' he asked.

'Awa' hame and read the Good Book,' said the garageman, who seemed to be muddled about the source of Beth's reference. Guffy looked puzzled, as well he might.

CHAPTER TWO

Winter was late beginning but when it came at last it arrived with a vengeance, as though the weather gods wanted to make up for accidentally giving us a long and lovely autumn. We braced ourselves. Could spring be far behind? the poet Shelley asked. We knew only too well the answer, that this far north and on a latitude as far from the equator as that of Cape Horn—yes, it could be a hell of a long way behind and it probably would.

Personally, I rather enjoy bad weather in limited doses. There is a perverse pleasure to be had from dressing appropriately and then going out to face the worst that the elements can throw at you, and an even greater pleasure in staying at home before a bright fire while the storm rages outside.

That is for myself, considered in isolation. But when you enter the world of dogs, different considerations arise immediately. I except Labradors, which are as near waterproof as a dog can be. But spaniels . . . Nature, I think, designed spaniels and sponges on the same day. Few dogs can get as totally saturated or look, when wet, as insanitary and second-hand and yet as pleased with themselves.

To make matters worse, snow is to spaniels as water is to fish. In the kennels we had our breeding stock. We had pups and young dogs in training. We had clients' dogs which had been left to be trained. And we had boarders, the dogs left by owners who had gone abroad for skiing holidays when they could have had better skiing, and much cheaper, at home. They all required exercise, those in training even more than the rest. (The dogs in the quarantine kennels still had to be fed, cleaned, mothered and kept free of little parasites, but at least walkies were strictly forbidden.)

A wet dog in an outside kennel is as prone to rheumatism and arthritis as its human counterpart. Even when aided by the drying cage which we had constructed and which could blow-dry two simultaneous spaniels while the next pair was being given a preliminary towelling and the previous pair was being brushed, our two kennel-maids were hard driven in a bad winter. As they themselves admitted, they could eat like starving tapeworms and not put on an ounce. There was no call for anorexia nervosa at Three Oaks Kennels.

Training—my speciality—had to continue, somehow. The youngsters could be taught elementary obedience in the big barn but dogs at a more advanced stage needed space. In the conditions, retrieving lessons were very difficult. Retrieving may come second in a spaniel's repertoire but it is a very important second.

Two days after the snow stopped falling, I was heading for the gate to the adjacent field

23

more or less accompanied by Accer (short for Acacia), a young black and white male springer. Beauty had returned to the world. The day was perfect. The wind had dropped and a low sun was throwing blue and golden shadows across the unmarked snow, turning the shrubs into strange sculptures and draping the branches of the trees. The world was muted. Beth's bird table was doing boom business.

The beauty of the day was not at the forefront of my mind. Accer showed promise but had proved slow to learn the to-and-fro hunting pattern of the springer in open ground, preferring always to lead the way, thereby putting up only game which would anyway have been put up by his handler. I had taken to walking a zigzag pattern until the penny had dropped at last and I wanted very much to keep it where it had fallen, but for the purpose I would have to find a place where the snow was shallow enough for brisk walking on both our parts.

Accer cared nothing for peace and beauty. He greeted the outing with enthusiasm, wanting nothing more than to excavate a stick or stone from under the snow and throw it in the air, hurling himself up and after it with abandon. I let him blow off steam.

To tell the truth, I was facing the outing with rather less enthusiasm. Accer was one of those maddening young dogs that can seem to learn a lesson only to have forgotten it by morning. Maturity would bring the remedy, I kept telling myself, and each dog must learn at its own pace. In the meantime, I dared not give up.

We had reached the gate and I was bringing Accer under control of a sort when I heard the sound of a vehicle on the far side of the house and then Beth's voice calling me. I turned back with, if anything, a sense of relief.

Beth met me at the back corner of the house. Like myself she was shod in wellingtons and clad in waxed cotton. Her cheeks were rosy. So also was her nose. She looked about eleven years old. 'Ben Garnet's arrived,' she said in a stage whisper.

I nearly turned around again. Even trying to drum the elements of his job into Accer was better than parleying with Garnet. But Beth obviously expected me to do my duty and I could hardly let her down.

'Kennel Accer for me?' The frost was still sharp and our breaths were steaming.

'Of course,' she said. 'Lunch soon. Don't be too long. And remember what you promised me. Come on, boy.' Surprisingly, Accer went with her.

I found Ben Garnet leaning against the bonnet of a new-looking Subaru estate which I had not seen before. He straightened up and greeted me with a smile as though we had always been the best of buddies. 'Good morning,' he sang out. 'How are you keeping?

No recurrence of the old trouble?'

I assured him that I was keeping well. I refrained from a reciprocal enquiry, preferring not to be assured of his continuing good health. He glanced towards the house but I was damned if I was going to invite him inside. 'What can I do for you?' I asked.

'Nothing that will cost you money,' he said. He spoke lightly, but I had a feeling that he was not joking.

'Yes?' I said. I waited.

'A signature.' He produced a green paper, apparently out of thin air. I recognized the Kennel Club's Form One. 'Your dog put my bitch up the spout.'

Beth's parting remark suddenly made sense. I had almost forgotten the incident at Lord Crail's shoot. Now it struck me that the other Lord had delivered Garnet into my hand, testicles first. 'I'm sorry about that,' I said. 'I can quite see that you have a problem.'

He looked at me sharply. 'I have?'

'You certainly have. Because I'm not signing.'

'But without your signature I can't register the pups.' He spoke as if explaining something simple to a child who had failed to grasp it first time around.

'That's right,' I said. 'You can't. Is that all you wanted? I have to get on.'

'Come on, now,' he said smoothly. 'You can't leave a neighbour in the lurch.'

'You're not my neighbour and I can.' To my eternal shame I was rather enjoying myself.

'But why?'

'For a start because you put them together deliberately, which makes it a self-inflicted wound. We were very down on self-inflicted wounds in the army. For another thing, because I've no way of knowing that she wasn't served by other dogs in addition to Horace.'

'That didn't happen,' he said. He was displaying the excessively frank and open expression of one to whom the truth is as alien a territory as the surface of Mars.

'You may know that,' I said. 'I certainly don't.'

'You can take my word for it.'

'If you were me,' I said, 'would you take the word of somebody with your reputation?' (I expected him to flare up at that. If somebody had said as much to me I would have hit out first and worried afterwards about my fitness for a fight. But Garnet never even blinked.) 'A third reason, if you really need one, is that I have a rooted objection to my bloodline being taken over and mass-propagated in competition with me.'

He was shaking his head, almost pityingly. 'All that I and my friends want is a handful of pups to train for rough-shooting.'

'And you'd sign an undertaking that none of them would ever be bred from or entered in field trials?'

27

His eyes gleamed and he nodded. I could guess just how much his assurance would be worth at a later date. 'In that case,' I said, 'I can't see why you want to get them registered.'

That new line of argument brought him up short. I saw his face harden. If I had not had such a dislike of him he would have had some of my sympathy. The Kennel Club, having destroyed several good working breeds by imposing unrealistic show standards, had gained a stranglehold on gun-dog competitions. Despite the fact that the first ever field trial was won by a springer/cocker cross ('sprocker' to the facetious), entries were only accepted for registered dogs of unmixed breeds, progeny of registered ancestors on both sides. If Cleo's pups were not registered, neither they nor any of their descendants to infinity could ever be registered; thus any kind of competition under the aegis of the Kennel Club would be out of court.

Personally, I disagreed strongly with the KC attitude and I had said so loudly, often and in print. Our present working breeds had been compounded, very successfully, from combinations of older strains designed to foster specific attributes and talents. To close the gene pool permanently was a guarantee that no improvement by out-crossing, nor the attendant hybrid vigour, could ever be obtained. It was and is a cul-de-sac philosophy. But however great my dislike of the Kennel

Club's short-sightedness, my dislike of Ben Garnet and his sharp practices was greater.

Garnet felt his way towards a new line of argument. 'I guess they'll have to be put down,' he said with a sigh.

'That's often the best way,' I agreed.

'Don't you care?'

'I care,' I said truthfully. 'I hate to see even new-born pups put down. But I'm still not going to be conned into letting a whole lot of Horace's valuable bloodline go begging.'

I was warmly dressed and booted but he was just out of his car. The breeze must have cut through his city clothes and the snow was definitely over the sides of his shoes. I wondered for how long I could spin out the discussion. I was pleased to note that his ears and fingers were turning blue but he was not going to give up. There was hard currency at stake. He shifted ground again. 'Of course, I would expect to pay a reasonable stud fee,' he said, with all the enthusiasm of one who is passing a kidney stone.

This was the first mention of a fee; and his interpretation of the word reasonable and mine would never coincide. I searched around for a figure which would be more than he would pay but not so much as to be fantasy—the sort of figure, in fact, which would drive him mad in the witching hours. 'One thousand pounds,' I said suddenly. 'Up front, now, today.'

There was a pause during which I began to

worry. He might well complicate the issue by agreeing to my figure. Both of us would know that it would never be paid. 'You get my signature after your cheque has cleared,' I added.

'You're mad!' he said at last.

'Pay the fee and I won't be the least bit mad,' I said. I started to turn away.

'Come on, now. A hundred. No pup, no fee.'

'Dream on! Resign yourself to having a litter of good working spaniels,' I told him.

'Be reasonable,' he said. That word again! Nobody commends reason so strongly as those who go against it.

'I am being very reasonable,' I said. 'Tomorrow, the price will have gone up. Substantially.'

He brandished the form in my face. Charm had failed for the moment. Now was the time for bluster. His face switched instantly from *bonhomie* to antagonism. 'Sign this bloody form,' he growled.

'No.'

'You'll be sorry. I, personally, will see to that.'

'Am I to take that as a threat?'

'Take it any way you like, I'm telling you that you won't get away with it. I'll have you in court first.'

'Do,' I said. 'And I can produce a dozen witnesses to swear that the mating wasn't any of my doing and that the difference in value of a good litter of pups of that breeding between being registered and unregistered could be a thousand of anybody's money. Except yours, of course.'

He let his fury show—not just in his face, but every line of his body stiffened. I could see him searching for the most cutting Parthian shot. He let a sneer settle across his face. It looked more natural there than his usual bland expression. 'Tell me, little man,' he said. 'What do you want to be . . . when you grow up?'

He threw himself into the driver's seat of his car and started off with a burst of wheelspin and a slither that nearly swung the tail into me. It would have looked accidental but it was absolutely deliberate. I watched him out of sight. If he should slide off the road or be stopped by the police, I would not have wanted to miss it. But I was doomed to disappointment. I went into the house. I could afford to ignore his parting words. He was at most five years older than myself, probably less.

I took off my many outer layers inside the back door and came into the large, bright kitchen which is the hub of the house and of our business. In the lobby I passed our two kennel-maids, Hannah and Daffy, who were on the way out with puppyfood. Hannah was looking scandalized but Daffy grinned at me. I gathered that my conversation with Ben Garnet had been audible indoors.

In the kitchen, I was greeted loudly by Sam,

31

who was in his high chair and being fed by Beth. Isobel, my other partner, was putting a plate of soup for me on the table where her elderly husband, Henry, was already seated. Henry is not a member of the firm but he is often around, helping, advising or just lending moral support. Home, for Henry, would have been a silent bungalow a couple of miles away, but here he could find companionship, banter and youth. Too many of his contemporaries, he said, had retired to the garden or the bowling green and allowed their intellects to atrophy. His body might be failing but Henry liked to keep his mind alive.

Isobel flashed her unsuitable spectacles at me. By strangers she could have been taken for any unassuming lady with no outdoor aspirations; but she is a qualified vet as well as being a naturally talented dog handler with a string of wins and several championships to her credit. She also has an encyclopaedic knowledge of gundog bloodlines and a computer program to back it up.

'Are you sure that that was wise?' Isobel asked, putting crusty bread beside the soup.

I found that I was ravenously hungry but I delayed long enough to ask, 'What can he do?'

'He could make a nuisance of himself, but that's not what I was thinking,' Isobel said. 'It seems to me that Horace is the perfect stud for Cleo. They both have Champion Knutsford Walfrey for a grandsire,' she said—reverently,

for she was speaking of the great and good—
'and you know what sort of a line he throws.
The rest of their pedigrees complement each
other. There's no eye trouble in either strain
and they both have low hip scores.'

The soup was very hot but I managed to
swallow my mouthful. 'So?' I said.

'So get after him. Say you'll sign the form
provided that you get, say, three pups of your
choice out of the litter.'

'Golly!' Beth said and Sam repeated the
word over and over. Even Henry shot his wife a
startled look. I had to agree with all three of
them. First choice of one pup is the customary
alternative to a fee. But, of course, that would
presuppose that the parties were on equal
terms. Perhaps Ben Garnet had outsmarted
himself.

I emptied my mouth again. 'You can put it to
him if you want to,' I said. 'I've had enough of
him. I may try it on if he comes back to the
attack.'

'When, not if,' Henry said. 'You know what
he's like. And I suggest that you warn the
Kennel Club to look very hard at your
signature if Ken Garnet's name turns up on a
Form One.'

*   *   *

As if the forces of nature were pursuing a plot
to drive out of their minds those sentimental

33

souls who yearned for a white Christmas, the first thaw came in late December. Instead of a white Christmas we had one that was sloshy, soggy and just plain wet. It was succeeded by a white New Year; only a few inches this time, but the frost that followed held the snow and kept it crisp while the roadsides turned grey and paths became pedestrian accident black spots. When a wind blew, the cold was bitter; but mostly it was a period of short, calm days with skies of an incredible blue above a white landscape patterned with black.

Three days into the year, I came back from exercising several young dogs on the Moss and glanced into the sitting room to find the message indicator on our answering machine blinking. We had put off that particular extravagance from year to year on grounds of cost, the inability of Beth and the girls to cope with gadgets and the fact that the house was very rarely empty. The new generation of tapeless answering machines had brought the rental of a phone with answering facility down to very little more than the rent of a naked telephone. With so many women in the house I had usually been the thrifty partner when telephones were discussed but, as soon as I was told that we had actually lost a sale because the client had been unable to reach us, I had insisted that the time for such a machine had arrived. It had soon proved its value. The snag was that nobody but myself ever looked at it unless they were specifically expecting a call.

This message was from a well-spoken Mr Hopgood, requesting a call-back. From the area code, he was calling from not many miles away.

Mr Hopgood proved to be resident in a small private hotel. A voice that claimed to be Reception (but was probably that of the maid of all work) put me through and he answered his phone on the second ring. I introduced myself.

'Thank you for calling me back,' he said politely. 'I'm told that you might have a trained or half-trained spaniel to suit me. My old dog had to be put down last week. Kidney failure.'

I commiserated and we discussed his requirements. He wanted a dog for rough shooting, some wildfowling and occasional driven days, preferred males, was not interested in competing and got on well with the exuberant type of dog. Accer came to mind at once. He had made great leaps forward, sometimes literally, in the past month. Some dogs seem incapable of learning and then develop with a rush. 'I have one that you might like,' I said. 'He's just seeing the light. You'd have to stay on top of him, let him see that you won't stand for any nonsense.'

'That sounds like my kind of dog,' he said. 'Some people prefer the shy and anxious type but while I've never owned one I don't think I could come to terms with it.'

I mentioned the price. That was the moment at which some enquirers made some excuse to break off the discussion, often promising another call which never came, but Mr Hopgood seemed to have a good idea of the present run of prices. 'When can I see the dog?'

I glanced at my watch. A client should never be given time to cool off or to tell his wife what he has in mind. If I grabbed an early lunch, we could still manage a couple of hours of daylight. 'Can you come over in about an hour?' I asked him. 'I'd prefer you to see him working. Bring a gun if you like.'

'Now that's what I call sensible,' he said.

I hurried into the kitchen to beg a quick snack. My share of the afternoon's programme was readily divided among the ladies. They knew as well as I did that just after the end of the shooting season was a good time to buy a dog but a hard time to sell one. A trained dog still unsold at that time was likely to remain, a hungry mouth and demander of attention, until the next season began to loom in late summer, without increasing in value.

Within the hour I was outside again, Accer at my heel and my gun over my arm. There was no sign of Mr Hopgood yet and I offered up a silent prayer that he had not changed his mind or had it changed for him by Mrs Hopgood.

The drive had been cleared of snow and I kept Accer carefully on it. He would undoubtedly get wet during our outing, but first impressions are important and a wet spaniel looks a ragamuffin. To while away a few minutes I sat him at the edge of the drive and walked along between the shrubs at the bottom of the lawn and the shoulder-high wall that bordered the road. Rubbish sometimes blew over the wall or was thrown over by passing litterbugs. This was a source of disproportionate annoyance to Beth, who managed to remain as proud of the garden as she was of the house despite the damage that any dog can inflict if left unsupervised for more than a few seconds.

Beth, I thought, had a right to be proud. She had worked hard on it. The deciduous bushes at the front of the border, now of course bare, were backed by foliage shrubs which provided the only relief in the frozen landscape. A viburnum was blooming pink in defiance of winter and the forsythia was budding nicely. The strip of bare ground against the wall where the snow had not found its way was fairly clear of rubbish, but what I took at first to be a clump of early crocuses turned out to be a small plastic carrier bag with multicoloured printing. Not only that, but when I picked it up in order to collect some of the few scraps of paper from among the dead leaves I found it stiff with dried glue.

Our end of Fife is not generally prone to trouble. To the south-west lie industrial and mining areas, but hereabouts the land is agricultural. Small residential colonies were only established by commuters using what were originally private ferries to Dundee; and even the construction of first the rail and then the road bridge across the Firth of Tay had little effect beyond the first mile or two.

Recently, however, there had been signs that the maladies bred elsewhere from unemployment and boredom were appearing in our quiet backwater and the more obvious of these was solvent abuse. Twice I had chased small parties of three of four glue-sniffers out of the barn. Only one of their faces had been known to me, which comfortingly suggested that even those small numbers had had to congregate from further afield.

I had little doubt that Tom Shotto was the ringleader. The others had seemed to have themselves under control and had offered me only impertinence and verbal abuse. On the second occasion young Shotto had been as high as a kite and ripe for violence, but when I made it clear that I recognized him and knew his identity the others had hustled him away. He was a tall lout, too lean even for his light build, with a spotty face and a round head covered only thinly with a haze of pale hair.

My musings were interrupted by the arrival of a car. I tucked the bag between the gatepost and the wall and forgot about it.

Mr Hopgood—Charles, as he introduced himself—was a well-built man in his forties, cheerful of manner and evidently very fit. He had a ruddy face, large but with disproportionately small features which gave him a slightly owlish appearance. His voice was deep and with a neutral accent although as I became tuned to it I thought, correctly as I learned later, that I could detect a trace of Edinburgh. He was sensibly dressed for a country walk through the Scottish January with flat cap, tweed coat, breeks and leather boots. He bent down to pull Accer's ear and the spaniel accepted the greeting with a violent wagging of his docked tail and latter end followed by an attempt to jump up which was instantly checked. The omens were good.

'If you don't mind walking a mile or so,' I said, 'I can show you how far he's progressed. This end of the Moss is a morass but the far side's passable.'

'We can take my car,' he said. His Isuzu Trooper looked almost new. Accer took to the back without hesitation. We got out at the mouth of a rarely used track and let the dog dismount. He wanted to race around and play.

'Call him to heel,' I said. I handed over a stag-horn whistle. 'This is the whistle he's been trained to,' I explained. 'It helps a dog to settle in if the same whistle goes with him.' I might have added that it also sells a lot of expensive whistles, but I kept that to myself.

We unbagged our guns. He had a very nice Cogswell and Harrison but I was not ashamed of the Dickson. We were in thick cover as soon as we moved off. Even in midwinter, that part of the Moss was sheltered by scattered clumps of spruce interspersed with gorse bushes and the dead remains of grass and reeds which had been drawn up into fallen brushwood.

'Tell him to "Get on",' I said.

Charles Hopgood repeated the age-old words. Accer shot away and vanished into the conifers. 'He's going a bit far ahead, isn't he?' Charles said doubtfully after a few seconds.

'Trust me,' I said. 'And him. He knows exactly where we are. He's taught himself to travel a figure-of-eight pattern which covers the ground very well. I don't know what gave him the idea, but it works.' Something black and white flashed through the bushes in front of us. 'If you want to see him, give him the "Turn" whistle. Two peeps.'

Charles gave two peeps on the whistle. The black and white streak came from behind this time, zipped almost over our toes and vanished again.

The Moss is trafficked by dog walkers and steadily poached, and I was using it again for dog training now that we had lost Foleyknowe, but an occasional pheasant still found its way there and decided to settle down. Accer homed in on a large cock among a tangle of dead grasses and sent him up with a whirr and an angry clocking.

'Yours,' I said quickly. The bird was on his

side.

Charles was caught off balance by the sudden explosion of the bird and the sun was against him. He fired too late, low and behind, and swore under his breath. The bird gained height, set its wings and glided from sight.

We started moving again. 'Better call him on,' I said. 'He'll stay sitting until you do.'

Peep-peep. Whoosh!

We were forced apart by an almost impenetrable thicket of gorse—although Accer seemed to ignore it as he hurled himself through. When we met up again, I said, 'Believe it or not, he can keep going at that pace all day.'

'What it is to be young!' Charles said. 'I like this dog. I think we can do business.'

Peep-peep. Zoom!

'Let's keep going,' I told him. 'I want to see you two get on the same wavelength. A common understanding now prevents cross-purposes later.'

Further on, we came into more open ground where thin snow, marked by the tracks and droppings of rabbits, lay between widely scattered clumps of gorse. I had Charles direct Accer by hand signals, trying to bring out their common language of movements, limited vocabulary, whistles and tone of voice. Even in midwinter there were rabbits which had rashly taken shelter in clumps of gorse which, overlying rocky ground, allowed no digging of bolt-holes. Accer bolted one, sat tight while Charles rolled it over and then fetched it to his hand on command.

A little later we came to the small pond at the centre of the Moss. It was open water where the feeder stream entered but the rest was thinly coated with ice. A lone mallard drake got up. My shot caught it over the land but it came down in the water. Accer swam for it, breaking the ice with his chest where he met it, and brought it out, this time favouring me with the retrieve. He shook himself, producing a rainbow in the low winter sunshine.

'I'm satisfied,' Charles said. 'We have a deal. No, back off, you silly sod,' he added to Accer. 'I'll fuss with you, when you're dry. Captain Cunningham—'

'Mister,' I said. 'And call me John.'

'John, then. You don't consider him fully trained?'

'He's coming along,' I said cautiously. 'Basic obedience is there and the elements of retrieving and hunting, but I still intended to work on his memory and marking and teach him to use his nose a bit more. He has a good nose but he still prefers to mark his game or be handled onto it.'

We started back towards the car. Accer, pleased with himself but knowing that work was over, trotted ahead. A wind had sprung up and was driving pellets of frosted snow into our faces. We hurried towards shelter.

'I'm only here for a day or two this time,' Charles said. 'And I can't take a dog where I'm staying for the moment. I take up my new post in six weeks' time. Could you keep him here until around then and give him his final polish? Then we can spend the spring and summer getting to know each other.'

It was a sensible programme from his point of view and remunerative from mine. As we chatted, I gathered that he was taking up a senior non-academic post with one of the three local universities and had come up to check up on the building of a house.

'I was offered a puppy from your stock,' he said suddenly, 'but I didn't want to waste most of next season training a novice—and then possibly getting it wrong.'

'Whose pup was that, then?' I asked.

'The man I've bought the site from. Garnet. He says he knows you.'

I nearly said that Garnet only thought he knew me. But it was not my business to utter warnings. What was more, Garnet was quite devious enough to have sent a stranger to trap me into making slanderous statements so that he could put pressure on me under threat of legal action. 'The pups are born, are they?' I asked.

'Seven of them. They look good. But I gather there's some question about their registration?'

'Some,' I said. 'Did Garnet tell you about that?'

'My builder had heard it on the grapevine. Garnet didn't say anything.' He sounded surprised and I thought that I could detect the first signs of doubt in his voice.

We arrived back at the car. Accer hurled himself over the tailgate. I dropped my game carrier with the rabbit and the duck onto the floor behind the front seats and he got in hurriedly out of the wind.

'How much is Garnet taking for the pups?' I asked.

'More than enough.' Charles mentioned a figure which was indeed more than enough. It would have been more than enough even if the pups had been registered. It seemed to me that Ben Garnet was painting himself into a corner. But he had painted himself into corners before and come out clean and shining and with the paint unmarked.

CHAPTER THREE

After a few more minutes of fussing with a delighted Accer, Charles Hopgood wrote his cheque and departed. As I handed the dog over for drying and kennelling he was holding his head high. I could have sworn that Accer knew that his status had improved from kennel stock to client's dog in training.

I was hardly into the house before Lord

44

Crail's head keeper, ex-RSM Fergusson, was on the phone and enquiring whether I would be free to shoot in a few days' time. Remembering Ben Garnet, I asked who would be along.

He knew what I was about and I heard his chuckle. 'This isn't His Lordship's day, this is mine,' he said.

That was different. Traditionally, the last shoot of the season belongs to the keeper; his guests are the beaters and pickers-up who have served all season for the love of it, the promise of the 'Keeper's Day' plus perhaps a fee which would be a tiny proportion of what they could have earned elsewhere. (And woe betide the shoot manager who breaks with that tradition. Next season, he will be lucky to recruit beaters averaging more than one leg apiece.) Ben Garnet would certainly not qualify for a invitation. I accepted hastily. A shoot run by a keeper for his own guests, without interference from the shoot's proprietor and after his need to conserve birds has passed, can be the best of the year.

'Saturday, then,' he said. 'Nine a.m. at the bothy. Fetch Mrs Cunningham along, if she'd fancy bringing yon Lab of hers. There'll be bree, beer, sasters and rolls. If you want ocht fancier, ye'll hae to bring it yoursel'.' Mr Fergusson, who liked to set a good example, was a careful speaker when Guffy could hear but in the boy's absence would lapse into the broad Scots of his early days.

After accepting with thanks, I hurried to check with the rest of the firm that it was all right. It happened that that weekend we had no other commitments. Rex, Daffy's husband, was home from the oil rig, so she was taking the Saturday off; but Isobel and Hannah expressed themselves happy to run the place between them, with back-up from Henry if needed.

If we had had an inkling of the events which were already germinating, we would never have gone to the shoot. But life is composed of a million things that one doesn't know for every one that one knows.

That Thursday, for example, we did not know that there was a message on the answering machine. Our telephoning was conducted almost entirely on the wall-mounted cordless phone, which usually lived in the kitchen but was as often in the pocket of whoever was around the house or garden at the time. A quick response to a ring obviated the need to wait through my voice telling callers to 'speak after the tone'. As it happened, nobody had looked into the chilly sitting room to see the little green light flashing.

And on that Thursday night a traffic policeman from Cupar came to our door to say that a man had been knocked down by a hit-and-run vehicle and found unconscious between the village and our gates. Had we seen or heard anything unusual? Lights for instance? We were able to assure him that from

46

dusk until his arrival, just before we went up to bed, we had seen and heard nothing. Henry and Isobel had driven home along that road just after six and, when we phoned them, were sure that there had been no unconscious man lying on or near the carriageway at that time.

Nobody told us that the injured man was Ben Garnet.

And so, on the Saturday morning, Beth and I set off in the car, with Jason and Blossom and the two cockers in the back. It was another crisp January day, the air so dry that one seemed to see every pebble on the furthest hill. There was a surprising amount of police activity at the roadside before the village but we took it as a sign that the victim of the accident had died and that the case had become one of manslaughter. Nobody told us that the doctors had been adamant that Ben Garnet's injuries had not been inflicted by a vehicle but by what one of them defined as 'a whack on the head'.

With only a mile to go we overtook a solitary cyclist, head down and struggling to make haste up a gradient. 'Was that Guffy?' I said.

'Probably. He's living with an aunt in our village. Didn't you know?'

'How would I know?' I asked reasonably. 'I'm not included in the gossip machine. Should I give him a lift?'

'We couldn't lift his bicycle as well. Not with dogs in the back.'

'True. So he'll just have to be late.'

The beaters were gathering in strength at the bothy. They raised a cheer when Guffy came panting in at last to meet the restrained fury of the ex-RSM. On more formal days, Guffy was in charge of the game cart; but on this occasion the function of the tractor and trailer would be replaced by two pick-ups belonging to the beaters and Guffy was needed for the beating line.

We moved off in good time.

At Foleyknowe on Keeper's Day, the ground had been virtually swept clean by the guests working in three teams so that at any moment one team was beating, one was standing and the third was already in transit to the next stand. While Mr Fergusson's shoot did not go quite so far over the top, nevertheless it was soon evident that a brisk pace was to be kept up and that the number of drives which His Lordship usually managed to put into the day would at least be doubled.

But our participation in the day was short lived.

Beth and I walked on the first drive. I had the two cockers with me and the little dogs bustled and burrowed through the cover with enormous zest. If I could keep them steady at the next week's trial, we would be in with a good chance. On the second drive I was a standing Gun, not far from the small loch, with Beth as picker-up well behind me. I had returned the cockers to the car and had Blossom sitting beside me as a test of steadiness. Mine turned out to be the 'hot seat' and I had eight birds down before the beaters appeared and the whistle sounded for the end of the drive. Blossom had never budged an inch and I was satisfied.

We prepared to move off for the pick-up, but there was a gathering of beaters near the last fence and somebody seemed to be waving in our direction. I thought that I had heard a squeal and I hoped to God that nobody had peppered a dog.

'Will you do the picking-up?' I asked Beth. 'Take Blossom with you. I'll go and see what's wrong.'

'To hear is to obey,' she said brightly, shouldering the canvas game-bag. 'I think there's only one to find. The rest are in the open.'

I left both dogs with her and went to join the throng.

The pundits of the gun-dog world are united in recommending that a dog is always lifted over barbed wire. It is almost the only subject on which they agree. I have gone along with them in theory but with reservations, because that advice is not always practicable. One function of a gun-dog is to retrieve birds which have fallen far off, thus covering many times the distance that a man could reasonably be expected to walk; another is to seek for birds which have fallen out of sight. An owner who would accompany his dog as far as the furthest fence might as well, if gifted with sharp sight and a good nose, do the job himself. Additionally, some dogs are too heavy to be lifted by some owners.

Most dogs become adept at crossing fences. Smaller dogs may seek a gap and wriggle through. Lightly built dogs will make a single leap, sailing high above the top strand. Some of the more heavily built dogs develop a knack of jumping onto and off the topmost wire, almost never, by some miracle, damaging their pads on the barbs.

Such a dog was Jumbo, a huge Labrador/golden retriever cross belonging to Joe Greystone. Joe had started life as a mason and bricklayer and had done some work for me on occasions, but he now spent his time as site foreman and drainlayer for a small builder.

Jumbo had come to grief on a fence which was topped with new wire, shining and sharp. Joe and another man were holding him still. Unbalanced and possibly unsighted by the large pheasant in his jaws, he had missed his footing and landed with all his weight on a barb. He was trying to struggle up and the sound he made was pitiful. Such accidents usually entail no more than a tearing of the skin, but it took only one glance to see that Jumbo had not only ripped his skin. The abdominal wall was also torn and several inches of intestine, luckily undamaged, protruded. There was an unpleasant amount of blood.

I was not a vet but the situation was not quite unknown to me. 'On his back,' I said. 'One man to each leg. Keep him still and for God's sake don't let him lick. Does anyone have anything we can use as a bandage?'

'Mr Fergusson's gone for the first-aid box,' Joe said. There was more anxiety in his voice than he would have shown over an injury to himself, and rightly so. 'Can we get him to Mrs Kitts?'

'Let's do that. She's at Three Oaks today.' It occurred to me that Jumbo's chances would be improved if Isobel was forewarned and the surgery was prepared. I looked around the faces and picked out Guffy. Surprisingly, I caught him in a huge yawn. 'Phone my house, Guffy,' I said. I quoted the phone number. 'Tell Mrs Kitts that we're bringing in a patient.'

Guffy dithered.

Mr Fergusson arrived back with his Land Rover and climbed stiffly out in time to hear what I said. 'Get going, boy,' he told him.

'From your house?'

'You'll be quicker to go down past the wee loch and along the side of the field to the Stouriden road. There's a phone-box there. That'll be best. Here. Take this.' He took a Phonecard out of his wallet and pushed it into Guffy's hand. 'You know how to use it. You've

51

made calls for me before.'

Guffy gaped as though he barely understood the words, but eventually he nodded and turned away. After a few yards he broke into a shambling run.

There were several big bandages in the ex-RSM's first-aid box and he had brought the remains of an old, torn-up but clean sheet. First I had to coax the intestine back through the stomach wall. Not without difficulty I managed to lift and manipulate the slippery membrane until the grey-green gut slid through and out of sight. I would have given a lot for a needle and thread but my guess was that a quick trip to Isobel's surgery would be worth more than a wait while a suture was fetched. I used up all Mr Fergusson's wide bandage in the hope of holding the lot together.

'Right,' I said. 'We need a coat to carry him in.' My first impulse was to offer my own; but the wind had a cutting edge. I had been sadly underweight ever since my sickness and was more sensitive to the cold than ever before in my life. Moreover, Beth would have hit the nearest roof if she had caught me stripping off while there were strapping younger men around. 'Any offers?' I enquired.

'I guess it'll have to me mine,' Joe said. 'Seems only right, like. What do you reckon? Will he be all right?'

'Of course he will,' I said stoutly. I was only offering comfort and Joe probably knew it.

We worked Joe's waxed coat under the dog without too much difficulty. Jumbo seemed to have discovered that effort equated with pain. At each corner, a man held the coat with one hand and Jumbo's leg with the other and thus we managed to move him gently, still inverted, into the back of the Land Rover. With Joe on one side of him and one of Joe's mates on the other, he was well stabilized.

Guffy came panting back from the direction of the loch, looking distraught. 'It's no' there,' he said. 'It's bloody gone!'

Ex-RSM Fergusson was not going to tolerate bad language or sloppy reporting from his subordinates. 'Don't swear,' he said severely from the Land Rover's driving seat. 'And what's gone?'

'The phone-box.'

Mr Fergusson spared a moment for an amused glance around the gathering. 'Don't be daft. It can't have.'

'It bloody has!'

'You must have looked in the wrong place.'

Guffy usually faced the world with a placid smile which quite disarmed his critics, but for some reason this caught him on the raw. He stamped his foot. 'I did not! There isn't a wrong place. I looked just where the phone-box was yestreen. It's gone. Somebody's nipped it. Or else it's bloody walked,' he added defiantly to Beth, who had just joined us.

This time, Mr Fergusson let Guffy's

behaviour go for the moment. There were more important issues. 'Somebody run and phone from my house,' he said. 'Then the rest of you may as well shoot on. Charlie, take charge. We'll set off in the Land Rover and get back when we can. And I'll deal with you later,' he added to Guffy. 'Vanishing bloody phone-boxes!'

'It's gone, I tell you,' Guffy said plaintively, his spurt of temper over. 'And who's swearing now?' he shouted after the receding Land Rover.

Beth had arrived with the missing bird and all three dogs. We decided to follow on. We had only a few minutes' walk to our car. In keeping with its function as an ambulance, the Land Rover was moving slowly. I decided that we could easily overhaul it. When we emerged onto the public road, out of curiosity I turned away from home towards Stouriden, a matter of no more than half a mile.

As it turned out, Guffy was right. The phone-box which had stood on a grassy triangle within sight of the row of cottages had vanished. The base remained, adorned by the sole of a shoe. Some wires protruded from a pipe in the ground and there were signs that the tarmac had been lifted and relaid not far away. Otherwise it was as though the phone-box had never existed.

Shaking my head, I turned and drove after the Land Rover. Truly the ways of British

54

Telecom were mysterious indeed.

* * *

We caught up with the Land Rover before the gates of Three Oaks and followed it up the drive. Police activity in the road outside seemed to have broken off.

As we parked, I thought that the hard-packed snow over the gravel in front of the house seemed to be rather full of cars but I was too concerned over Jumbo to pay them much attention. I simply assumed that the cars belonged to clients, prospective clients, disappointed shoppers or owners visiting pets boarded or in quarantine. Saturdays could sometimes be busy without being profitable.

Isobel had come out of the house to meet the convoy. With her was Daffy, the kennel-maid who usually helped her in the surgery when help was required. (The other kennel-maid, Hannah, was quite unperturbed by dog dirt but inclined to turn up her toes at the sight of blood.) The message had got through because both of them had donned white coats. Daffy's bizarre hairdo contrasted strangely with her surgical garb.

Isobel shot me a look which seemed intended to convey some warning or other, but she was carrying a loaded hypodermic syringe and she climbed into the back of the Land Rover without further explanation. The need to relieve pain and to prevent Jumbo causing more damage by struggling was paramount.

Two men in overcoats were trying to gain my attention. By now, there were more than enough people to handle Jumbo so I turned to the newcomers. I saw Mr Fergusson give them a look as if recognizing not the men but the species.

'Captain Cunningham?'

'Mister Cunningham,' I said for the hundred thousandth time. My army career ended when I fell desperately ill and I see no reason to continue calling myself 'Captain' and several good reasons why I should not. But my name must be associated with that rank in the innards of some badly advised computer and, however firmly I try to eradicate it, from time to time it emerges again like flame from a smouldering fire.

'Mr Cunningham, then. And Mrs Cunningham?'

'Yes,' Beth said.

There was challenge in her tone. She had sensed something that I had missed. I came alert and looked at the speaker. He was a burly man, looking more so in a thick overcoat. His head was square. His face was highly coloured and being rather flat with a pair of obtrusive front teeth it had a babyish look. All the same, something in the expression suggested strength. His companion was less bulky and seemed altogether more self-effacing.

'Inspector Burrard, Fife CID. And Sergeant McAndrew. We want a few words.'

The Inspector's voice was deep and slightly hoarse, almost rasping. I could have given him more than a few of the words he wanted, beginning with an exhortation to go a long way away and stay there. But a sedated Jumbo was vanishing into the house, borne and accompanied by a procession of anxious helpers, and there were no other immediate calls on my attention. So, instead, 'Do you have any identification?' I asked.

The look which he shot at and through me was intended to convey that I was only a member of the faceless public and had a bloody nerve to ask such a question, but he undid the top button of his overcoat and produced identification, complete with his photograph. It looked genuine. Sergeant McAndrew was similarly equipped.

I was feeling a little bit peevish, one of my rare days out having been spoiled by yet another dog unable to keep out of trouble; and my recent experience of the police was mainly of zealous officers wanting to know more than they were strictly entitled to ask about such matters as firearms certificates and the 1968 Act. 'What could we have done for you if we'd happened to feel like it?' I asked sourly. 'And whatever it was, let's talk about it somewhere out of the cold. Shall we go inside?'

As I spoke, I glanced towards the house.

Henry was watching anxiously from the sitting-room window but he sidestepped out of sight as the Inspector looked round.

'Your house seems to be as peaceful as Waverly Station on a holiday weekend,' Burrard said with sourness to match mine. He made it sound as though the house was full of terrorists, drug addicts or child molesters. His accent was faint but I thought that it was the near-Glasgow accent of Dundee. 'We'll be better off in the cars. Unless you'd rather come down to the station?'

We might have been more comfortable at the police station in the village, although knowing the old building I doubted it. In any case, something in Burrard's manner made me feel that I would rather be where my friends could see me from the windows of the house.

'The cars,' I said. Beth agreed.

The two cars that had brought the police were parked side by side. Another man, I presumed a driver, opened a door of a Range Rover for the Inspector and myself and then took the front passenger's seat, balancing a notebook on the dashboard. Beth and the Sergeant took the back seat of the humbler car. The Sergeant, it seemed, had to make his own notes.

Inspector Burrard produced a small tape recorder and started the reels turning. 'You won't mind us recording what's said as well as taking it down. We like to be sure that the statement we ask you to sign is exactly what you've told us.'

No question had been asked so I made no comment. 'What's this about?' I asked him.

'You don't have to say anything. But whatever you say will be taken down as well as being recorded and may be used in evidence.'

If he was tossing Statutory Warnings around, the matter was serious. But my conscience, on cursory inspection, was clear. 'What's it about?' I asked again.

'Would you care to make a guess?'

I could see that it was meant as a trap and a rather obvious one—unless the Inspector was especially subtle in which case the wrong answer would be to pretend not to see the obvious. I gave some thought to the question. 'Some traffic cops came here late one evening,' I said at last. 'I think it was Thursday, the night before last. We were given to understand that somebody had been knocked down by a hit-and-run driver near here. From all the sudden activity in the road this morning, I assumed that he'd died. Some people are only important once they're dead. Am I getting warm?'

'Barely tepid,' said the Inspector.

'I can't say that I'm surprised. I didn't see how a traffic accident could concern a detective inspector, but I couldn't think of anything else. You'd better tell me.'

Once again he avoided a direct answer. 'I think you know Mr Benjamin Garnet, of

Highhirst Farmhouse?'

'We've met,' I said cautiously.

'What kind of relationship did you have with him?'

This could be dangerous. On the other hand, my dislike of Ben Garnet was public knowledge. If something unpleasant had happened to Garnet, I might just as well reveal my true feelings by giving three cheers. I would not be alone. To try to hide my feelings would be more suspicious by far.

'I make damn sure that I don't have any relationship with him. If he's not a crook,' I said, 'he comes very near it. I try not to meet him. But he's never quite robbed me yet.'

'You've no call to resent him at all?'

'I wouldn't say that. He got away, by sharp practice, with the sporting rights to a shoot that we depended on for dog training. We lost the facility, some income plus all the work we'd put into it.'

'So you hated him?'

'That would be putting it rather strong,' I said. 'I despised him as I despise anyone who can't get by without ripping off his neighbour. He seems to pull a fast one, not just when he needs to but as a matter of principle even if he must know that in the long run it's going to rebound against him. Is he dead?'

'Why do you ask that?' the Inspector demanded.

'Because you suddenly used the past tense.'

60

Burrard looked both disappointed and surprised. 'I believe I did. A slip of the tongue. Am I right in thinking that there was some friction between you over his spaniel bitch?'

'Not on my side,' I said. Burrard waited. I decided that I had nothing to lose by going on. 'When his bitch was in high season, Ben Garnet put her in the way of my stud dog. It was a blatant, and successful, attempt to steal a valuable service. What he forgot is that it's no use to him unless I certify that my dog is the sire of the pups, for registration purposes. And I'm damned if I'll do it.

'Why not?'

I outlined for the Detective Inspector the same reasons that I had given Ben Garnet. He only grunted. For all I could tell he might have been signifying that those reasons were hardly grounds for thwarting a neighbour or, alternatively, that they furnished ample motive for murder. He leaned forward and glanced at the other car. My eyes followed. When I had looked across a moment earlier, Beth and the Sergeant had seemed to be having no more than a pleasant chat, but now I saw that she was looking anxious. A small but definite signal passed between the Sergeant and his superior, but I was unable to interpret it.

The Inspector sat back, looking pleased with himself. 'Tell me how you spent Thursday evening,' he said. 'The night before last.'

'Tell me why you want the information,' I

said, although I could have made a perfectly good guess. The Detective Inspector's manner seemed to expect the worst from me and made me want to give it.

'Would that knowledge affect your answer?' he asked.

'No,' I said. 'Of course not.'

'Then you don't need to know just yet. First you satisfy my curiosity and then I'll satisfy yours.'

Once again I felt that innocence was defence enough and that we might as well get the unhappy business over and done with. I wonder now how many innocents have talked their way into trouble, using the same reasoning. 'Mrs Kitts, my other partner, left with her husband to go home at about six,' I said. 'We took our evening meal a little later. One of the kennel-maids, the one known as Daffy, had gone off early because her husband's at home from his oil rig. The other kennel-maid, Hannah, ate with us and then went off to her room at the back to watch television.

'Beth went to get Sam, our son, ready for bed while I washed up. Then we both saw him into bed and I read him a story. When he fell asleep, around seven-thirty, we came downstairs.

'You're sure of all this?' he asked.

I watched a lone blackbird scavenging under the shrubs while I thought about it. 'I don't have a clear recollection of that particular

62

evening,' I said at last. 'I've given you our usual routine which, as far as I remember, is how Thursday evening went. Any departure from it would have stuck in my memory.'

'Go on.'

'I remember what came next. The sitting room was chilly. It hadn't been occupied that day. We couldn't be bothered lighting a fire to supplement the central heating. The television's in there but there was nothing on the box that either of us wanted to see. So we settled down in the basket chairs in the kitchen, as we often do if we're alone. Beth had a book and I was writing on my knee.'

'Writing what?' the Inspector asked keenly.

I sighed. 'I can't imagine what possible interest that can be to you, Inspector,' I said. 'But in fact I'm drafting a book about spaniel breeding, training, care and competition. It may never get published, but the existing books are beginning to date and I've already had a nibble from a publisher.'

The Inspector let me see that he found my literary ambitions supremely uninteresting. 'What else?' he said.

'Very little. About nine-thirty we had a cup of tea. An hour later, we were thinking of going up to bed. We keep early hours, Inspector; dogs don't lie in in the morning. Then—and this is how I come to remember Thursday evening— that's when two constables arrived at the door, wanting to know whether we'd seen or heard

63

anything unusual.'

'And had you?'

'Not a thing. I wasn't even aware of any cars going past. We don't hear them much through the double glazing or see the lights through our thick curtains.'

'I see.' The Inspector drummed his fingers on his knee. 'And you and Mrs Cunningham were together all evening?' he asked very casually.

'As far as I can remember, yes. Either of us may have gone for a pee . . .'

'But you didn't go outside?' he persisted.

I yawned. This was all very boring. 'Not that I remember,' I said. 'Bear in mind that until the officers came to the door it was an evening like a thousand others. I wasn't keeping notes or memorizing my movements.'

The Inspector raised his eyebrows. Then, leaning forward, he signalled to the Sergeant, who came to occupy the driver's seat in the Range Rover, which I took to be the Inspector's car. Beth, with several worried looks over her shoulder, went into the house.

'Mr Cunningham says that he was with his wife all evening,' said the Inspector.

Boredom was gone in an instant. 'That is not what I said,' I told him sharply, 'and you know it. Play the tape back.'

'No need for that just now,' the Inspector said. 'Plenty of time later. What did Mrs Cunningham say?'

64

The Sergeant looked almost apologetic. I gathered that he had no liking for a scene which had clearly been scripted. 'According to Mrs Cunningham, her husband went outside before nine o'clock. He was absent for about half an hour.'

'What have you got to say about that?' the Inspector shot at me.

I felt the blood rush to my face. 'I haven't "got" to say anything,' I retorted. 'But if Beth told you that that's what happened, she may well be right. I do sometimes go out for a last look at the dogs and there's a limit to how much original writing one can do at a sitting. I just didn't think that it had happened on the evening that the two cops from Traffic came in about the hit-and-run. I told you that I had no particular reason to remember.'

'I see,' the Inspector said. When I was a subaltern I had served under a company commander who had the same knack of putting disbelief into a tone of voice and the lift of an eyebrow. 'And while you were out, did you see or hear anything?'

'If I had, I'd have told your officers.'

'Those officers must have arrived shortly after you came in from your walk.'

'That's one reason why I think that my wife's mistaken about which evening I went outside.'

'I see.' The Inspector's voice held so much doubt that I could feel my colour rising. 'Mr Cunningham, would you have any objection to having your fingerprints taken?'

'None,' I said. There would have been no point in objecting. One way or another they would certainly obtain them. 'And now, I think that that explanation is due.'

'You're sure that you can't guess?'

I would have had to be as thick as a mattress not to have a fairly dependable idea by now, but I weighed my words carefully. 'Obviously something happened on Thursday evening. The only event I know about was the supposed hit-and-run between here and the village. My guess is that you have reason to believe that it wasn't accidental. And you asked about Ben Garnet. If he wasn't the victim, then I can't imagine where he comes into it.'

'There you are,' the Inspector said comfortably. 'You didn't need me to tell you after all. What would have brought Mr Garnet to this vicinity?'

'Your guess would be as good as mine,' I told him. 'Perhaps he was going to have one more go at persuading me to sign his form.'

'And could he have done so?'

I nearly listed a number of extraordinary events which would have had to take place before I could have been persuaded to sign the form. Instead, I said, 'No.'

'And you've nothing else to tell me?'

I said, 'No,' again.

The Sergeant had a portable fingerprint kit with him. When they had my prints safely

66

recorded, they entered their separate cars and departed. It was a safe bet that we had not seen the last of them.

CHAPTER FOUR

I washed the ink off my fingers in the empty kitchen and joined the crowd in the sitting room where a fire was burning and a party seemed to be in progress.

Surgery had been completed and the patient, I gathered, was expected to make a full recovery. Mr Fergusson, with Joe and Joe's crony, could have gone back to rejoin the shooting party. I thought perhaps that they were waiting for us to go with them, but it seemed that the visit of the police, flavoured by generous drinks from our sideboard, was of greater interest. Joe in particular had no interest in shooting without Jumbo being along for support while Mr Fergusson seemed glad of an excuse to take the weight off his feet. Even Hannah and Daffy, who should have been busy feeding or humanizing pups or cleaning runs, had joined the throng.

Every chair was occupied so I took a seat on an arm beside Beth. Her fingers, I noticed when she laced them with mine, still showed faint traces of ink. Henry, who had been doing the honours as he often did, poured me a glass

67

of Guinness. We seemed to have the makings of a good ceilidh. The fire had been lit in honour of the occasion although, between the central heating and the number of bodies present, the room was becoming uncomfortably warm.

'Well?' Beth said. All eyes were on me.

'The Inspector was remarkably unforthcoming,' I said. 'All I was able to gather was that Ben Garnet was the victim of the hit-and-run on Thursday night and that they think it was deliberate. I suppose he's dead.'

'That he's not,' Joe said. 'I'm working on Mr Hopgood's house, see, just across the field that Mr Garnet calls his paddock. We're making ready for the founds but we need a break in the weather before we dare pour the concrete. Mrs Garnet spoke to me as I was lowsing last night. She said they found Mr Garnet's car in the pub car park here but the police weren't letting her have it back yet. She asked me to give her a lift in my old van to go and see her man in the hospital.' Joe was a large young man and very strong and with a heart as big as himself. 'I waited and brought her back,' he said. 'Mr Garnet wasn't dead. She'd've said,' he explained carefully.

He might, I thought, have died later, just to please me. 'What did she say, then?' I asked.

'She said he'd an awfu' concussion. Just beginning to make sense, she said, and there's gaps in his memory, but they think he'll be a'

68

right in the end. Oh, and it wasna' a hit-and-run. They thocht it was at first but there was no vehicle in't at a'. He was hit with something. The doctors found a hell of a lump on his head and none of the other bruises and scrapes he'd've had if he'd been knocked down.'

Inspector Burrard had not told me any lies but it seemed that he had been far from frank. I wondered just how much damage might have been done. I have a faith, which sometimes seems to be misplaced, in the outcome of British justice and I had no fear of being convicted of an assault on Ben Garnet; but I knew that suspicion could lead to infinite time wasting, harassment and general nuisance, while if it went to the length of a prosecution there would be more of the same plus considerable legal costs.

Daffy stirred. 'I'll go and give the pups their second feed,' she said reluctantly. She looked at Hannah, who avoided her eye. Daffy went out, closing the door ungently behind her.

I took the vacated chair. 'You told the Sergeant I went out on Thursday evening?' I asked Beth.

Beth looked stricken. 'I thought you did. My God! Was I wrong?'

'I thought it was Wednesday that I went for a late stroll to see that the dogs were settled.'

'It could have been,' Beth said, frowning. 'Now that you mention it, I think it was.'

'Were you questioned?' I asked Hannah.

Hannah nodded solemnly. She was turning into an attractive young woman with regular features enhanced by a humorous nose. She and Daffy had at one time been at daggers drawn but I was amused to see that the original antipathy had been overcome to the point that Daffy was now helping Hannah with her make-up. Hannah would never have thought of green tinselled eye-shadow on her own. 'They asked me a lot of questions,' she said. 'I couldn't answer most of them. I said I didn't know whether you'd gone out on Thursday evening. Well, I didn't know what you'd want me to say.'

'Shall I phone the Inspector and set the record straight?' Beth asked me.

'No!' Henry said sharply. I felt Beth jump. 'It's too late for changing stories now,' he said more softly. 'Time enough to mention that you're unsure which day if they want a formal statement. Otherwise you'd only make him suspect collusion.'

'He'll suspect it anyway ... in addition to whatever else he's already suspecting. He seemed to know all about my dislike of Ben Garnet. You surely didn't tell him about that?' I asked Beth.

Beth and Hannah shook their heads.

Mr Fergusson chuckled drily. 'Aabody kens you canna' thole the man,' he said. Again, now that he was no longer setting a good example for Guffy, he had let down his guard and relapsed into his native dialect. 'You never speak to him if you can hold wide of him. Farivver he is, you're as hyne-awa as you can get. And, what's more, Garnet hissel's been going around and telling folk that you'll like him a damn sight less when he's made you sign his form about the pups.' He shook his head in lofty disapproval. 'You're no' alone, mind. There's hardly a soul for miles around will give him the time of day. It's a wonder the mannie's wife can abide him. A nice-like body she is.'

'She's loyal,' Joe said. 'If she hears him tell a lie, or somebody repeats it to her, she just says that it's only Ben's way.'

'Before he went out on Thursday night, what had Mr Garnet told her?' Beth asked Joe. 'Did she say?'

'Aye.' Joe looked at me. 'He telled her he was coming to see you. He said he was going to make you sign some paper about the pups. I'm sorry, Mr Cunningham, but that's what he told his wife and it's what she told the police.'

'Well, it beats me,' I said after some seconds of thought. 'He didn't tell her how he proposed to make me sign?'

'If he did, she didn't tell me,' Joe said.

The company looked solemn and sympathetic but I could guess what kind of stories would do the rounds.

Mr Fergusson and the two beaters left soon after that but Beth and I felt too disturbed to go back with them to what was left of the shoot. As he went out of the door, Joe stopped for a

71

moment. 'I'll not forget what you and Mrs Kitts have done for Jumbo,' he said. 'He's a'most as near to family as I've got.' With that for thanks he followed the others to the Land Rover.

'I thought that he had a brother or something,' I said 'But I know what he means.'

Beth went to recover Sam from his nursery in what had once been the spare bedroom while I returned the sitting room to collect glasses. The telephone cum answering machine was half hidden by one of Beth's indoor plants, a lemon-scented geranium, but as I reached for a used whisky glass I saw that the little green light was flashing.

'Have there been any incoming phone calls?' I asked Isobel.

She broke off her discussion with Henry. 'Not for a day or two, to my knowledge,' she said.

So it was probably a genuine message and not just the result of a call which had been taken while the answering function was switched on. I pressed the Play button.

An unnatural falsetto voice reached clearly to every corner of the room. 'You'd better sign that form about the pups,' it said, 'or something terrible's going happen. Just terrible.'

There was a long silence on the line, except for an intermittent background buzz as though the caller had a bluebottle in the room with him.

Despite the shock, my mind was still working.
The first thing that I did was to switch off the
answering function—otherwise, now that the
call had been played, the next incoming call
would have overlaid the message.

Henry and Isobel were staring. 'How long
has that been on there?' I asked the world in
general.

'No idea,' Isobel said. 'The telephone's been
very quiet for a day or two, or maybe three. It's
like that at times. It rings twenty times a day for
a week, and then nothing.'

'And I've been busy,' I said. 'I listened to a
message on Wednesday. I've been too busy to
look at the thing since then.'

'There's not a lot of point paying rental for it
if nobody listens to the messages,' Isobel said
loftily.

'It cost peanuts more than the phone
without the answering bit,' I said. 'But each of
us expects the others to attend to it. We'll have
to set up a routine.'

'Before you start one of your interminable
board meetings,' Henry said, 'may I point out
that the sooner you play the message to your
friend the Inspector the less scope he'll have
for suggesting that you put it there yourself as
a distraction.'

He had a point. I called the headquarters at
Kirkcaldy and they promised to contact the

Inspector by radio. As it turned out, he and Sergeant McAndrew were still at the village police station where our local bobby was assisting the investigation by providing a room and cups of tea. By the time that Beth had returned, listened to the message and dispatched Sam to exercise the pups with Daffy—a chore which he always enjoyed—the two officers had returned, bringing the local man with them.

We waited while they listened intently to the brief recording. This time, I remembered to hold down the save key so that the message would not be overlaid. 'It's not very clear.' The Inspector glanced round our faces, seeking inspiration. 'Is there always that buzzing in the background?'

'I hadn't noticed it before,' I said.

'When did this message arrive?'

'We don't know. Some time after Wednesday.'

Henry cleared his throat. Henry is an elderly man with a modest manner but he was once a moderately big wheel in the City. I don't know how he does it, but when he indicates that he intends to speak, silence falls. I have a similar knack but it only works with dogs.

'I seem to remember that the little green light was flashing twice,' he said. 'Doesn't that mean that there's another call which hasn't been listened to?'

I played the threatening message again and

left the machine running. After another long silence, the caller hung up, to be followed by a routine message from the owner of a poodle in the quarantine kennels, wanting to be assured that her darling was alive and well.

'That doesn't take us very far,' Isobel said.

'It does, you know,' I retorted.

The Inspector listened at one shoulder and Beth at the other while I called the lady, set her mind at rest and apologized for the delay in ringing her back. She told me that she had called on the afternoon of the previous day. She had no idea at what time. I thanked her and disconnected.

'The only time the house was empty yesterday afternoon,' Beth said, 'was between about two and two-thirty.'

'So there we are. The threatening call was made some time between Wednesday and those times yesterday afternoon,' I said.

The Inspector nodded without commenting. I could see that his mind was busy coming to terms with the challenge to his favourite theory. 'You don't recognize the voice in the recording?' he asked.

'Have a heart, Inspector!' Isobel said. 'It said very few words in an obviously disguised voice.

'On top of which,' Henry said, 'the real culprit could very easily have had somebody unknown to us relay the message.'

'Or even have had somebody put the words on tape and then played it over the phone,' said

Beth.

'I'm afraid that's so,' the Inspector said. 'I'll have our technicians try to clarify the message and see what else they can tell us. They may even be able to make a useful voiceprint, though I wouldn't count on it. I'm afraid I'll have to take your phone away with me.'

'You can't do that,' I said quickly.

He bridled, his suspicions revived. 'Why do you object?'

'You're welcome to borrow the instrument provided that you give me a receipt,' I said. 'But as soon as it's unplugged, you'll lose the message. In fact, I'll transfer it to tape now in case of a power cut.'

The Inspector looked at his Sergeant, who nodded. 'Do that,' the Inspector said. 'And I'll have a technician come here with some rather more sophisticated equipment and transfer—'

The interruption came with a slamming of doors and a patter of feet. Daffy burst into the room with Sam in her arms. She was a weird enough sight in her calf-length leather skirt over what looked like army boots, her synthetic leopardskin duffel coat and with the usual fluorescent stripe in her hair—silver that day, I remember. The wild look in her eye turned her into something from a horror movie. I saw the Inspector flinch.

My heart was in my mouth at the thought that some disaster had overtaken Sam. But Daffy dumped him hastily in Beth's arms and I could see that although he was upset he was unhurt.

'Come quickly,' Daffy said. 'Something's happened to Accer.'

'What?' Isobel asked forcefully.

'Don't know.' She looked pointedly at Sam. Beth, as though by accident, covered Sam's ears. 'Looks like poison,' Daffy said.

Beth gave Sam to Henry and the rest of us followed Daffy outside. Sand, put down to save us from skidding in the icy conditions, gritted underfoot as we hurried along the path. The kennels were arranged in blocks of four and Accer's was at the furthest corner. The spaniel was lying in the middle of the small run. Vomit stained his usually snowy muzzle and the ground around him. Hannah, caring nothing for the mess, was kneeling down and cradling his head. As we arrived I thought that he tried to move his tail. His eyes were open and they sought mine. A spaniel's eyes can be the most expressive in the world. They can express love and trust. And fear . . .

I forced myself to kneel and add my comfort to Hannah's.

Isobel, more practical, was looking around the run. 'If he ate something,' she said, 'he ate all of it. Damnation! Get him into the surgery and I'll do what I can, but not knowing what it was doesn't help. From the blue colour of his sick it could be slug pellets. And he's brought up what could have been a piece of steak. I'll have to wash him out and assume slug pellets—that's the easiest poison for anyone to get hold of without leaving a record behind them. Come on.'

Accer was light, much lighter than Jumbo. I picked him up in my arms and ran to the house. Shudders shook his small frame as though he were trying to vomit again, but nothing came. Isobel was ahead of me, opening doors. In the surgery, which had been converted out of a former scullery, Jumbo, still snoring, had been moved to a basket in a corner. I put Accer on the steel table.

'Now go,' Isobel said. 'All of you. Daffy can stay and help me.'

Hannah and I cleaned the traces of Accer's vomit off ourselves in the kitchen and then joined the others in the sitting room. The fire was dying. I put on a couple of dry logs and gave it a stir. Any scrap of comfort helps to counteract a worry or a sorrow. Henry had vanished with Sam—for a walk, we discovered later. Henry could always be counted on to do the right thing. The Sergeant, I noticed, was also absent but he came in a minute or two later and nodded to the Inspector.

'Samples have been taken,' Burrard said stiffly. 'You will be informed of any result obtained.' He cleared his throat. 'Tell me, how could somebody from outside get at a dog in that way?'

'Easily,' said Beth. 'We keep to a fairly

78

regular routine and sometimes there are quite long periods when there's nobody out at the front. Anyway, somebody in the road beyond the wall could lob a piece of meat as far as the runs.'

'That assumes that he didn't care which dog was poisoned.'

'You heard the message,' Beth said. 'He probably didn't give a damn.' Her voice broke on the last word, turning it into a curse. She turned away and sniffed in her handkerchief. I wished that I could do the same. I had developed one of my fondnesses for Accer.

'I don't know who did it,' Hannah said huskily, 'but I'll kill him if I can.'

She left the room but turned back immediately as Isobel came through from the surgery, pulling off her latex gloves. 'I lost him,' Isobel said.

There was the sound of a car outside. Looking out, I saw that Charles Hopgood had come to visit Accer. The late Accer.

*　　　*　　　*

Detective Inspector Burrard, no doubt, could see as well as we could that the poisoning had to be connected with the threatening message and that the message itself had some connection with the attack on Ben Garnet. He never made any open accusations but it seemed to me that he had convinced himself that a smokescreen was being put up by one or more of us. He would very much have liked to keep us separated and yet under supervision until each of us had been questioned and our statements recorded.

He went outside but we could hear him clearly. Over his radio he requested and then demanded support which, it was soon clear, would not be forthcoming as long as Ben Garnet continued to make a recovery. The Inspector was sure that the case was one of attempted murder while his superiors preferred to regard it as one of common assault. Even in the police force it is only human to believe what one wants to believe.

Burrard's tactics and attitude then perforce underwent a quick change and he asked us, quite politely by his standards, to remain segregated and incommunicado. But to no avail. We scattered and he was left to catch who he could for questioning and to hope in vain that the others were not discussing recent events. Isobel insisted on leaving the house in order to collect samples of Accer's vomit for independent analysis; Daffy and Hannah had the best of reasons for resuming the ongoing work of the kennels; it was my sad duty to explain the disaster to Charles Hopgood; Beth was adamant that everybody who had missed lunch must be fed forthwith and she would not be deterred; Sam had made up his mind that he was not going to be parted from Daffy; and

Henry was trying to mediate between the various parties and calm the rising hysteria. The Sergeant went off with Isobel to witness the taking of the unlovely samples and then to take her statement.

I broke the news to Charles in the sitting room, still littered with the aftermath of the morning's company but now deserted except for ourselves and the Detective Inspector. Burrard may have felt that in Charles he had a character in the drama who was unaware of the plot to date and who might therefore let slip whatever we might be concealing. If so, he was to be disappointed.

On the whole, Charles gave a creditable impression of one who is taking the news well. I saw him close his eyes for a moment as if in pain or prayer. 'But why would anybody do such a thing?' he asked huskily.

'We don't know,' I said. 'We can only guess.' I kept one eye on Burrard as I began to explain about the threatening message, but the Detective Inspector made no move to object.

Charles decided to answer his own question. 'Either a sick mind or an evil one,' he said, 'to be so desperate for one spaniel as to kill another one just to ram home a threat.'

'That's exactly what we were thinking. Of course, I'll refund the purchase price,' I told him.

'No need for that,' he said gruffly. 'I'm sure that no blame attaches to you.'

'I had him insured.'

The approximation to a smile which Charles managed to produce could have been used to scare away witches. 'So did I,' he said.

'Then we'll let our insurers sort it out between them,' I said. 'It seems that neither of us should be out pocket. I can't offer you another Accer—he was the last of his litter— but we have some rather younger dogs coming along. They'll be ready by next season.'

Emotions chased each other over his face. It lit up, then clouded. Finally he laughed at himself. 'I'm not sure that I'm ready yet,' he said. 'It hasn't sunk in. I not even sure that I quite believe it.'

'Would you like . . .' I nearly said *to view the remains* but checked myself in time, '. . . to see him?' I finished.

He shook his head emphatically. 'I'm being foolish. When you suggested another dog, I started wondering if it wouldn't be disloyal to Accer. Then it came to me that I'd only met him once and known him for about an hour.' He sighed gustily. 'It shows you how a dog can get under your skin in that short time. Kipling warned us against "giving your heart to a dog to tear".'

'He was right,' I said. 'But I do it all the time. Not to be recommended, in my job.'

'All the same, perhaps it's why you're good at it,' he said. 'Common sense says that I should choose another dog, forget Accer and get on with my life. But if common sense ruled our emotions it would . . .'

'Be a very different world?'

'Exactly.' He sighed again. 'I don't promise anything but, yes, show me another one if you like. Perhaps it's akin to getting back on the horse that threw you.' He paused and gave a small shiver. 'Liver and white, if you can. I don't think I could take to another black and white dog so soon after hanging my hopes on poor Accer.'

'These are cousins of Accer,' I said. 'There's a black and white dog not yet spoken for.' Suddenly I couldn't wait to get out of the house. 'Come on then,' I said. 'It'll take both our minds off it.'

'Just a minute,' the Inspector said sternly. He had been a silent spectator, probably wondering what on earth got into so many of us that we should value a dog so high. 'I must ask you to remain here for the moment.'

It seemed to me that Burrard was only trying to reimpose his dominance. But too much of my life had been spent obeying ill-considered orders. 'Tell me why,' I said.

'I shall want a statement from you.' I could tell that even to himself it sounded weak.

I felt my temper beginning to slip. The stresses of the day were telling on me. 'You'll get it when I'm ready,' I told him. 'For the moment, we have been trying very hard to tell you everything that led up to the time when the poisoned dog was found,' I pointed out with some force. 'If you care to believe that we were pulling the wool, that's your problem and not ours. From that moment on, you were present. Meanwhile, our lives have to go on. I'm not going more than a couple of hundred yards away. Come with us if you wish. Otherwise, take your own statement or go and bother somebody else for half an hour but leave us alone.'

I waited.

Burrard thought for a moment and then decided to give in gracefully rather than force a confrontation. 'Very well,' he said with dignity.

'Come on, then, Charles.'

We collected our coats. In passing the kitchen we somehow found ourselves each with a mug of soup in one hand and a hot dog in the other. When Beth makes up her mind that somebody should eat, there is no avoiding it.

Charles paused outside the back door. 'I wouldn't push the Inspector too hard if I were you,' he said.

'You're probably right. He puts my back up. You do still want a male dog?' I asked, as we trod the paths through the frosted garden.

'I've always preferred them. I don't know why. Perhaps it's just that they don't come into season just when you need them most.'

'This was a litter of seven, of mixed colours.' I racked my memory. 'The dam and one paternal grandsire were champions. I think

84

that's right—Isobel can fill in the details. Four were sold as pups and I still have two of those here in training for the owners. The other three I'm bringing on to sell as trained or part-trained. One's a bitch and one of the dogs is black and white, leaving you a choice of one.'

'Which saves a whole lot of decision making,' Charles said.

'It's just yes or no,' I agreed. 'He's just such another forceful character as Accer. He's been showing up well in early training and if you come back at a less fraught time I can let you see his dam working and put him through his paces. His full name's Cedar of Three Oaks but we call him Sid for short.'

'If I take him—and it's a big if—I'd call him Hob. Short for Hobson. Hobson's choice.'

'He's still young enough to accept a change of name,' I said.

At the kennels, Daffy and Sam were letting some of the younger pups exercise themselves on the grass. We gave her our empty mugs.

'First,' Charles said, 'show me where Accer was kenneled.' We walked to the far corner, not far from the wall and the road. From the signs, Isobel and the Sergeant had finished and Daffy had already cleaned up. 'An easy throw,' Charles remarked.

'He needn't have entered the property at all,' I agreed.

Charles nodded. 'What's in my mind is that he needn't have been after Accer in particular or getting at me through him.'

We turned back. Sam detached himself and ran to take both our hands.

Charles seemed flattered but kept his mind on the business in hand. 'That's rather a relief,' he said.

I wondered why he should be expecting any such hostile action, but this was not a good time to ask. Sam was capable of taking in every word and repeating them. 'I think you can take it that it was a blow struck at my partnership,' I said.

Charles would have asked more questions but I discouraged him with a headshake and a downward glance.

Sid came to stand up against the wire of his run, his docked tail flicking like a windscreen wiper. When Charles entered the run, Sid took one look, sniffed one sniff, rolled onto his back and whined in ecstasy as Charles stooped to rub his stomach.

Charles looked round at me. 'You must have put him up to that,' he said. 'May I take him for a walk?'

'I come too?' Sam said quickly.

'If that's all right by your dad,' Charles told him.

I decided that Charles was both sensible and trustworthy. 'Come back to the house for a lead,' I said. 'And a ball or a dummy. You can try him out with a simple retrieve or two. Stop if he gets bored.' Then I wondered if I was not being rash. 'You'll be careful,' I warned, 'and don't go beyond the field.'

'I understand,' he said. He was looking serious. I thought that the wound left by Accer's death, which had hardly begun to heal, might be the best possible guarantee that he would be vigilant.

I hurried ahead of them, back to the house. Whatever Detective Inspector Burrard was being told, I wanted to know about.

Henry, well wrapped against the chill of the day, was pacing about outside the front door, keeping an eye on Daffy and watched in his turn by Burrard's driver. Henry caught my eye and raised his eyebrows in the manner of one who wants to confer.

'Moment,' I said.

I fetched a lead and a canvas dummy for Charles. Beth was being interrogated by Detective Inspector Burrard in the kitchen. Each of them signalled to me to stay in the room. I ignored them for the moment. Burrard might have insisted but he was distracted by an incoming radio message which he seemed to find interesting and I slipped outside again.

'Follow the footprints round the house right-handed,' I told Charles, pointing the way. 'You'll come to the gate into the field.' I decided to reinforce my message. 'If you see anybody at all, come straight back in a hurry. We simply don't know what's going on.'

Charles nodded. He had fetched a heavy stick from his car. 'They'll both be safe with me,' he said.

From the set of his jaw and the way he gripped his stick I was inclined to believe him. 'And take your time,' I said. 'I don't want somebody not a million miles from where we are at this moment to know more about all this than he has to.'

'I understand.'

As they moved off, Sam gave me a knowing look. I avoided his eye and joined Henry.

'The reason I'm freezing my balls off out here,' he snarled, 'instead of toasting them in front of your fire, is that somebody should be keeping watch and I don't see any other volunteers. Think about it. There was a threatening message on your phone. Shortly after it was put there, Ben Garnet was assaulted, perhaps murderously. And that happy but unsuccessful event was followed by the murder of one of your dogs.'

'I'm aware of all this,' I began.

'But had it occurred to you that, as Beth has been pointing out over and over again to the Inspector, Ben Garnet looks very like you?'

'No it hadn't,' I said indignantly. 'It still hasn't. He doesn't.'

'Don't get on your high horse. There are some superficial differences,' Henry admitted. 'Only one of you looks intelligent. But the two of you are about the same height and the same skinny build. You favour the same sort of clothes. Even your voices are not dissimilar.

88

Your outlines, in the dark . . .'

I avoided rising to the bait about intelligence and instead gave my attention to the thought that Henry was expressing, which was new and a very long way from being welcome. My skin felt as though ants were walking up my back, through my hair and behind my ears. 'You think he was swatted in mistake for me?'

'And so does Beth. And if that Detective Inspector doesn't soon agree, he's wearing mental blinkers. Think of it that way round and the elements begin to make a little more sense.'

'How has the Inspector been reacting to that idea?' I asked.

'Nobody knows. He doesn't seem sure himself. To be fair, it's not his job to react until all the facts are in. You could always ask him what he thinks.'

My chances of getting a straight answer from the Inspector were slim. Perhaps there was a more direct method. Burrard's driver, if that is what he was, was standing at the corner of the house and looking vacant.

I approached him. He was an athletically built young man. In jeans and a thin sweater he seemed impervious to the cold and something told me that it might not be wise to resist being arrested by him. For all his relaxed expression I sensed that he was alert. 'Are you just waiting?' I asked. 'Or on watch? Or on guard?'

He smiled. He still looked half asleep. 'You could say all three,' he replied.

'You know what's been going on?'

He nodded. I waited. 'A threat, an assault and a poisoning,' he said at last. I glanced at his lapel. No radio. Without seeming to look at me he showed me the small radio in his left fist.

'Help could take half an hour to respond,' I said. 'If anything happens, yell bloody murder. We'll come running.'

'That might not be the wisest course, even if you are ex-army.'

'But my son—' I began. I looked round and with a small spasm of fear realized that Sam was out of my sight.

'—is in the field with the other gentleman,' he finished for me without even glancing in that direction. 'They're hidden by the small conifer at the moment but they're there. Quite safe.'

Henry had followed me. I led him to one side. Charles and Sam came into view. 'It seems that the Inspector at least considers it a possibility,' I said. 'Let's go in.'

'Gladly,' Henry said.

The Detective Inspector was still with Beth in the kitchen. He seemed to have been subjecting her to formal questioning but I noticed crumbs round his mouth. Despite the crumbs he still had the remote air of one who expects to be told tarradiddles and so takes nothing on trust. I noticed that our local bobby, Constable Buchan, had been called into service as a note taker to supplement the Inspector's little tape recorder. They were clustered round the central table.

'Mrs Cunningham has given me some more of the background,' the Inspector said, looking round at me. 'As I understand it, your land around the house and kennels is crossed and recrossed frequently in the normal course of business but that there are times when nobody would see an intruder. An enemy would only have to be patient. Would you go along with that?'

Henry and I had settled into the basket chairs by the range with fresh cups of tea. 'That's about the strength of it,' I agreed. 'The runs are all locked with combination padlocks, for what that's worth. We rely more on the dogs themselves as being the best intruder alarm. We have microphones hidden among the kennels and linked to speakers in the house.'

'The dogs don't bark if the arrival is somebody they know?'

'Not usually. They didn't bark at you today because you were with us. But a lump of meat could be thrown over the wall. I never knew a dog yet that barked at a lump of meat. You must have noticed that Accer's kennel was one of the few within easy throwing distance of the wall.'

The Inspector's face showed a trace of irritation. 'In daylight? In full view from the village street?'

Henry chipped in. 'The village street is

91

almost half a mile away,' he said, 'and only one or two staircase windows face this way. This weather doesn't encourage people to be pottering in their gardens. Do you really think that anyone would notice the movement of a walker's or a cyclist's hand at that distance? Or a car stopping for a moment?'

'You're assuming that the poison was intended for no particular dog.'

'We're assuming rather more than that,' Henry said. 'We're assuming that the poisoner wouldn't have cared very much if the poisoned meat had fallen on the ground outside the runs.'

The Inspector thought it over, his stern expression at odds with his strangely juvenile cast of features. 'I don't follow,' he said at last.

'Look at it in sequence,' Henry said. 'A message threatens unspecific disasters. Somebody who could easily be mistaken for Mr Cunningham gets coshed in the dark. It would matter little whether the next incident was the poisoning of a dog or the discovery of poisoned meat near the runs. It adds up to scare tactics, the result of which was to have been an intimidation of Mr Cunningham and his partners.'

'But by whom?' the Inspector asked with an air of triumph. 'The only person with a motive for the message is still in hospital.'

'And you, Inspector,' Henry said, 'are assuming that everyone behaves in a rational manner although you must have seen the contrary a thousand times in the course of business. Any one of the prospective purchasers of Mr Garnet's puppies may well have set his heart on a pup of that particular breeding, properly registered to permit competition and breeding.'

'And there's nobody can get as fanatical as some of the dog-people,' Beth added. 'Nobody!'

There was the embryo of a smile on the Detective Inspector's face. 'So I have been noticing. You make your theory sound very logical—' he began.

'Because it is logical,' said Beth.

'—and it might hold water. But we haven't yet found the weapon Mr Garnet was struck with. When we do, it's almost bound to show traces of its use—blood takes a lot more washing away than the public thinks and Mr Garnet bled quite freely. One would also expect fingerprints.'

'But?' I said.

'But indeed.' The Detective Inspector smiled grimly. 'But the general public is becoming very wise about prints. Very probably the attacker wore gloves. Or gripped the weapon through a plastic bag. And we found a polythene bag at the roadside, Mr Cunningham, with your fingerprints all over it.'

I was struck dumb for a moment by the notion that my fingerprints on a carrier bag

93

should be regarded as somehow incriminating. Before I could reply we were interrupted by a commotion and a shout from the officer outside. The Detective Inspector and Constable Buchan were quick off the mark but, despite the other officer's warning, I was ahead of them. Beth trailed the field and Henry followed in his own time.

To my relief, the uproar had, after all, nothing to do with Charles Hopgood and Sam. There was some thrashing around in the shrubbery and two figures shot out of the gateway. A third emerged from the bushes, struggling in the grip of the other policeman.

We all came to a halt in a ragged group. 'Well, well!' I said. 'Tom Shotto! Inspector, have you met our local glue-sniffer?'

Burrard examined the youngster without any sign of pleasure. 'Apparently not,' he said. 'Not this one. What were they up to, Gribble?'

The officer—Gribble as he was now identified—stood his captive in front of the Detective Inspector and gave him a small shake, just to remind him who was in charge. 'There were three of them,' he said. 'They were hiding behind the bushes, but it's a transparent sort of cover at this time of year and they didn't even have the sense to keep still. I couldn't see what they were up to, but I'd have bet my pension that it was nothing their mothers would approve of. They may only have been planning a little solvent abuse, but from the way they were watching the house they were up to no good.'

'We weren't watching the house, you bugger, we was watching you,' Shotto whined. He was a gangling and underweight school-leaver. His unkempt hair was pale and, perhaps by intent, stuck up in spikes. His appearance was not improved by watery eyes, nor by the fact that he was prevented from shaving his vestigial beard by a nasty case of teenage acne.

'Well? Why were you watching my officer?' Burrard demanded. 'What were you up to?'

'Naethin',' Shotto said defiantly.

It seemed to me that I was in the market for a useful red herring. If I could turn the Inspector's mind in other directions than mine, I might have peace to get on with earning a living. 'They may have been settling down for a jolly session with the glue,' I said. 'On the other hand, I've turfed them off this property in the past and been threatened for it. I wouldn't put it past any of them to poison a dog or to try to knock me on the head, out of sheer spite.'

Young Shotto squawked indignantly and embarked on a spirited denial but, because this was only a protestation of innocence repeated over and over in slightly differing words, it carried very little conviction along with it.

We had rushed outside without waiting to put on coats. Apart from Gribble, who seemed frostproof, only Tom Shotto in his grubby but quilted anorak was adequately dressed and I for one was beginning to feel my body heat being sucked away. Henry had already retreated into the warm and Beth was calling to me from the front door. I turned back towards the house.

'You might compare his fingerprints with those on the carrier bag,' I threw over my shoulder.

It dawned on the Detective Inspector that he too was becoming frozen. 'Bring him inside,' he said.

Beth moved aside to let me in and then resumed her position in the doorway. She had a point to make. 'You are not bringing that scruff into my house,' she said firmly. 'God knows what he'd leave behind.' She backed away from the doorway, rubbing some warmth into her upper arms.

Burrard hesitated, but evidently he could see some force in her argument. 'Very well,' he said. I could hear him clearly through the open door. 'Buchan, you interview the boy in one of the cars. If you can get any sense out of him, take a statement. Find out where he was at the time of both incidents. Then check.'

'And in between, sir,' Buchan said. 'Do I let him go?'

'Depends how well he accounts for himself. Use your judgement.'

The exchange was innocuous but I was amused to note how much attitude could be conveyed by tones of voice. It was clear that

Burrard had no great faith in Constable Buchan's judgement while the Constable, as well as disliking his superior, was not taken with the idea of being cooped up in a small car with young Shotto. All three sentiments had my sympathy.

The Inspector followed us hastily inside and the door was closed.

I chose the kitchen again as being the warmest room and joined Henry, who was thawing himself out in one of the basket chairs. Beth settled again at the table.

'Let me get this straight,' said Burrard. He towered over us, mostly, I think, to get close to the source of warmth. 'First of all, explain how your prints came to be on the carrier bag.'

'Why wouldn't they be?' Beth demanded hotly. 'It could be a carrier bag my husband brought home with some shopping.'

'Hold it,' I said. 'Maybe it could and maybe it couldn't. Inspector, are we talking about a blue carrier bag with black and white lettering?'

I saw him prepare to pounce. 'What if we are?' he said.

'I found that bag against the wall behind the shrubs. It must have been left over from some previous sniffing session,' I explained. 'I picked it up, meaning to use it to collect some scraps of paper that were blowing around nearby.'

The Inspector nodded, half satisfied and half disappointed. 'There were traces of what seems to be dried glue in the bag,' he said. 'So that was the bag that they—or somebody—poured glue into and then sniffed vapour from the bag. It's what it may have been used for later that concerns us. Are you suggesting that Shotto's fingerprints may have been on the bag from a sniffing party? Or that he used it to grip some weapon?'

'Either or both,' I said. 'That's for you to decide. I'm only explaining how mine got onto it.'

Burrard frowned. 'There were no papers in it when it was picked up.'

'I only lifted it as something to do while I waited for Charles Hopgood to arrive. He turned up before I could get started, so I tucked it between the gatepost and the wall.'

'Securely? Or could it have blown away? It was picked up near where Mr Garnet was struck down, between your gate and the village.'

'I tucked it in quite firmly,' I said. 'And there's been very little wind since then.'

Henry, who had been listening in intent silence, stirred so that his basket chair gave a sudden creak. 'And what wind there has been,' he said, 'was in the opposite direction.'

Detective Inspector Burrard stood looming silently for a while. I thought that he was considering the implications of the carrier bag, but it seemed that Charles Hopgood's name had started a train of thought. 'Mr Hopgood?'

he said. 'That's the client whose dog was poisoned? We only have his London address. Do you know where he's staying? I must see him again as soon as possible.'

'That shouldn't be a problem,' I told him. 'Charles Hopgood is still here. He's considering another young dog as a possible replacement for the one that died. They've gone for a walk in the field to get to know one another. My son went with them.'

Burrard's eyebrows went up. 'He went for a walk with your little boy?'

'It seemed to be a chance to keep Sam away from all the fuss and flap.'

'Is there any reason we shouldn't?' Beth asked sharply.

'None at all,' Burrard said. 'Excuse me.' He went out of the room, trying to move quickly while trying not to be seen to hurry.

We looked at each other, puzzled and slightly perturbed.

'I'll go and see what he's on about,' I said.

'All right. I'll leave it to you,' Beth said. 'This time, wrap up well.'

I went through the other door, collecting my sheep-skin coat from the back lobby, and came out beside the tiny shop from which we dispense dogfood and equipment to occasional customers.

We were usually so careful about leaving Sam with a stranger. But Charles was not a stranger. Charles was a friend. We all liked him. I held myself back from breaking into a run.

CHAPTER FIVE

I caught up with the Inspector at the corner of the house. He had abandoned any pretence at sang-froid and had backed young Gribble against the wall by what seemed to be sheer force of panic. 'I thought you were supposed to be keeping your eyes open,' he ground out.

Gribble had given ground but he refused to be perturbed. 'They're open, sir,' he said. 'Wide open.'

'The man and the boy who went into the field. Where are they?'

I had had time to move around and use my eyes. 'They're still in the field,' I said. 'If you come a little bit this way, you'll see them.'

He took one pace to the side and leaned a little, and the figures emerged from behind a large straw bale. The larger human figure put up a hand. I heard a whistle and the spaniel, little more than a dark dot against the mixed snow and stubble, came streaking towards them. The Inspector closed his eyes for a moment and then, rather than acknowledge the anticlimax, nodded as if to say 'Just testing' and hurried to the gate.

I followed on quickly. Sam seemed to be in

100

good spirits, but if the Inspector thought that there was any reason why Charles should not be allowed out of sight with my son, I wanted to know. It might also signify that I should not take Charles's cheques or even sell him a pup.

Sam, I noticed, had been throwing the dummy while Charles kept Sid under control. (Sam, the product of his environment, had developed a remarkable throw for a four-year-old. In the garden, one had to be sure to point him away from the windows.) When they saw us approaching, they walked to meet us. Sam had fast hold of Charles's hand and Sid was tight to the man's heel. The three seemed to have been enjoying themselves.

Ignoring Inspector Burrard except for a token nod, Charles was speaking to me before I was within ten yards. 'He's good, but he's no Accer. He's very slow to respond to hand signals.'

'He's younger than Accer was,' I reminded him. 'He's just arriving at the age for rapid progress. I'd expect him to do most of his learning during the next few months.'

'Good point,' said Charles.

'Good point,' echoed Sam, tasting the words.

Detective Inspector Burrard put a stop to further chitchat by telling Charles firmly that he wanted a word with him. I decided that Sam should be out of earshot and detached him.

'Your boy,' Charles told me, 'has been lecturing me on how to handle a dog.'

101

Henry had been given a watching brief by Beth. He was waiting by the gate rather than commit himself to the shallow climb. I took the lead from Charles, attached it to Sid's collar and gave it to Sam. 'Take this, go to your Uncle Henry and help him to put Sid in his kennel,' I told Sam. The two of them scampered happily off across the hard ground. 'Don't take everything that Sam tells you as gospel,' I said. 'We differ on one or two of the finer points. Check with me first.'

Charles laughed. 'So far, his advice has been better than much that I've been given over the years.'

Inspector Burrard had been waiting for the moment when he could speak with a good chance of having Charles's attention. Now he waited for me to leave them together but I had every intention of hearing what was about to pass between them, either at first hand or later. Burrard glared at me and waited.

Charles saw the by-play but had his own idea. 'You've been open with me, John,' he said. 'I can guess what's coming and you must be wondering what it's about. You may as well hear it now rather than have to take my word for it later.'

'If you say so,' I replied. 'But let's not stand and freeze while I hear it.'

'Right,' Charles said. We set off for the house.

Burrard was not going to be put off any

longer. 'Mr Hopgood,' he said. 'I want to know the nature of your quarrel with Mr Garnet.'

'You do, do you?' Charles said without slowing down.

'Yes I do. And if you want to be interviewed in the presence of comparative strangers, that's up to you. After the attack on Mr Garnet—you know about that?—we found your message on his answering machine, saying that he'd already made one mistake and if he didn't return your call immediately he'd be making another one.'

'And what's wrong with that?' Charles asked tartly. 'It hardly adds up to a quarrel, would you say, John?'

'An argument,' I suggested.

'Those words might or might not have been a threat,' Burrard persisted. 'They were enough to start some enquiries rolling. Some of the answers have just reached me. Last Sunday night you called at Mr Garnet's house. His wife says that you were angry about something but she doesn't know what.'

Charles was not one to show anger but I could hear a trace of irritation in his voice. 'She told you that? I told her exactly what I was angry about.'

'Now tell me,' said Burrard. 'Because this morning you called there again in a similar mood.'

Charles gave a shrug and swiped with his stick at a snow-girt weed-head. 'This morning was when I heard for the first time that

103

anything had happened to him. And in between, I was in London and can prove it.'

'I still want to know what the quarrel was about.'

Charles was silent until we were in the sitting room with our coats off. I put a couple of logs on the still smouldering fire. The Inspector and I took seats as near to its warmth as we could and began to thaw out again.

Charles took a seat on the couch. 'I may as well tell you,' he said. 'You can find out easily enough. When I made an offer for some land—'

'The site for your house?'

'Correct, Inspector. At that time, a rectangle was pegged out in the paddock. It enclosed several fine trees and the makings of a good garden. But, of course, the bargain was concluded on the basis of a dimensioned drawing. The plan had a note to the effect that the locations of the trees shown on the plan might not be to scale, but I thought nothing of it. You see, at the time, I hadn't heard of Mr Garnet's reputation.'

Detective Inspector Burrard only nodded. It seemed that Ben Garnet's reputation was not unknown to the police even if his activities were more or less legal.

'Oh dear!' I said.

Charles flicked an eye at me and looked a little less grim. 'That just about sums it up. The architect's drawings seemed to fill up more of the site than I'd expected,' he continued. 'I assumed that I'd been deceived by the scale and that houses always seem to get bigger in relation to the site.'

'Other way round,' I said.

'I realize that now. It was only when the builder came on site and pegged out his boundaries that I realized that the site was smaller than I'd been led to believe. Garnet's pegs had disappeared by then and you couldn't even see the holes. But as my solicitor explained, even if the pegs had still been there they would have had no bearing unless Garnet had assured me in front of witnesses that they demarked the site. Otherwise, it was only my rash assumption and one which I could easily have disproved if I had cared to measure the boundaries for myself.

'To make it worse, several fine trees were now outside the boundary and Garnet had told my builder that he intended to take them down for the sake of selling the timber. He may have been bluffing—the removal of the trees would have damaged his outlook almost as much as mine. There was a hint that if I paid him the value of several fine hardwood trees, they would remain up. Or I could buy more land— at developer's rates.

'The last straw was that my deal with Garnet included permission to connect to his sewer, which ran under the line of pegs at one side of my site; but the new position of the boundary meant that I had some yards of his land to cross to reach it and my solicitor reported that Garnet wanted more money for the way-leave. And to crown it all, as if there was not the least tension between us, he followed up by inviting me to join what he airily referred to as "his" shooting syndicate. He seemed to think that that would heal all wounds. Can you believe it?'

He was looking at the Inspector but I decided to answer for both of us. 'Very easily,' I said.

'That he'd choose to make a quick buck and at the same time make an enemy of somebody who was going to be his next-door neighbour?'

'I wouldn't believe it of anybody else,' I said, 'but for Ben Garnet that's about par for the course. He seems to believe that anything more above board is sissy.'

'In that case, there must be hundreds with sound motives for catching him in the dark with something hard and heavy.' Charles looked at the Detective Inspector again. 'But however much the man had annoyed me, you'll surely see that, even if I had been here and not in London, I would have had nothing to gain from Garnet's death.'

But Burrard, it seemed, did not see anything of the sort. 'Point One,' he said, 'you might not have needed anything to gain—anger is often sufficient. Point Two, the blow is not always struck by the man with the motive. I'm not saying that there was an accomplice, but the possibility is there. So much for your defence of alibi. Point Three, Garnet didn't die. The attack may have been meant only to intimidate him. Point Four, and alternative to Three, he might have been meant to die. You might have hoped to get a better deal from the widow.'

'And a pretty feeble hope that would have been,' Charles retorted with spirit. 'You can check with the lady. When I saw her this morning, I found that her husband had left her under the impression that the deal was already concluded. She thought that I'd called round to leave my cheque and when I tried to correct that impression she made up her mind that I was trying to pull a fast one, taking advantage of her husband while he was in hospital. Either that, or she's a better actress than I give her credit for. *She* called *me* a swindler.'

'You have now been taken to the cleaners by a professional. Welcome to the club. So what will you do?' I asked curiously.

He shrugged. 'I shan't join any syndicate that has him for a member,' he said, 'that's one thing certain. For the moment the other matters are in the hands of my solicitor. If he can't find a loophole, well, I may pay for the trees but I'd rather double the cost and lay my own sewer and build my own septic tank before I'd put one avoidable penny into that man's pocket—' He paused and looked at the Inspector. 'Or attack him,' he added.

                    *   *   *

I left them together for the Inspector to ask his
routine questions while I gave a hand with the
inescapable chores of the business. The peak of
the trialling season was almost on us. The
freezing weather had at least reduced the
burden of wet and muddy dogs; on the other
hand, in most years we would have avoided
having pups in January. We had no control over
the family planning of bitches left as boarders,
but our Viola had failed to conceive from a
mating the previous spring and had been put
back to stud in the autumn. The result was a
litter which seemed to be ten times the work of
a litter born in summer when the pups could
have been left to play in the sunshine.

The light was failing when I met the
Inspector on the doorstep. 'That will be all
tonight,' he said. 'We will doubtless be back in
the morning.'

I looked around. Gribble was already seated
at the wheel of the Inspector's car and Sergeant
McAndrew was getting into his own. 'Just a
holy minute!' I said. 'We've had a threatening
message, somebody's been clobbered on our
doorstep and you were almost witness to a fatal
dog-poisoning. You're not just going to walk
off?'

He looked at me, his face a blank. 'What did
you have in mind?'

'Does crime prevention not fall within your

remit?'

I seemed to have caught him on the raw because even in the poor light I could see that he flushed. It did not seem to be my day for winning friends and influencing Detective Inspectors. 'We simply do not have the manpower to mount a guard,' he said stiffly. 'Buchan will be told to keep an eye on the place.'

'And where is he now?'

'He just went off duty.'

Before I could put up any arguments he was into his car and away.

There was a pale van on the tarmac so I was not surprised to find Joe in the kitchen along with everybody else. The whole party, eight souls at a quick count including Sam, seemed to be enjoying a combination of what was either the lunch that we had missed or a rather early dinner combined with the usual knocking-off session of drinks and a discussion of the day's doings.

'Burrard refuses to leave anybody on guard,' I reported.

'That was to be expected,' said Henry gloomily. 'He thinks that one of us may have clobbered Ben Garnet and that some or all of us are covering up, which is particularly irritating when we haven't even had the pleasure of doing the deed.'

Beth glanced down to be sure that Sam was not following our discussion but he was absorbed in a game with his building blocks. 'Shouldn't somebody be out there?' she asked.

I checked that the loudspeaker, linked to the microphones at the kennels, was on. When I turned up the volume I could hear the rustle of bedding and one of the dogs, Samson I thought, grumbling to himself. 'The dogs will tell us if anybody approaches,' I said. I took my place at the scrubbed table and began to eat ravenously. Beth nodded approval. There were cans of beer of an unfamiliar brand on the table and a glass was poured for me. I guessed that Joe had come bearing rich gifts.

'The dogs won't tell you if somebody lobs more poisoned meat over the wall,' said Henry.

'Somebody can lob from the road all he wants to,' Daffy said. 'It won't do us any harm provided we pick it all up in the morning before we let the dogs out. We've moved them out of any kennels within throwing distance of the wall. It meant some doubling up but the dogs don't mind.'

'What do you call throwing distance?' I asked. A young woman's throw could fall far short of that of, say, a cricketer.

'Daffy threw a ball from the road,' Hannah said. She never usually touched beer but she had a glass of it in her hand. Joe must have been persuasive. She made a throwing gesture and slopped beer across the kitchen floor. 'Oops! She threw it a lot further than I could have done. Then we doubled the distance.'

That seemed safe enough. 'It'll do for the moment,' I said. 'But somebody could approach from the fields. We can't keep watch at night and still do a day's work. Should we hire a security firm?'

'You could,' Charles said. 'But from my experience of them, you might get a report at the end of the month, saying that a man had been observed throwing poisoned meat into one of the runs. I once received a report that welding cylinders had been seen in the courtyard, beside an open manhole, and pipes disappearing in the direction of the strong room. That had been in the small hours of the morning a fortnight before the report. Luckily it was only somebody working on the central heating.'

'If it's any help . . .' Joe began, 'I live in a caravan with my half-brother. There's neither of us married and we're both in the building trade, so it suits us well enough. We can put the 'van wherever it's handy for whatever job we're on. It's just over the hedge from Mr Hopgood's house this moment. But it'd be no bother to bring it here and park it right by the kennels. Then we'd be right on the spot if somebody had another go at you.'

'Would you do that?' Isobel said. 'The lights work off a sensor, so between them and the dogs you should get ample warning of any intruder.'

'That sounds good,' said Joe. 'My half-brother doesn't start work on site yet—he's a joiner—and he stays up half the night anyway. Could you give us mains electricity?'

'No problem,' I said.

'And you can come in for baths and food,' said Beth.

'And no charge for the work on Jumbo,' Isobel added.

'I was hoping you'd say that,' Joe said cheerfully. 'I'll away and fetch the caravan now. I may be a while. If Dave's not there I'll have to wait for him. Otherwise he'd be getting in a tizzy and calling the police to tell them the caravan's been nicked.'

'Finish your meal first,' Beth protested.

Joe pushed away his half-emptied plate. 'I'd better go and catch Dave before he sets out on a round of the pubs. There's more snow forecast.'

'Which is a fair guarantee that it won't come,' Henry said.

'Maybe. But nobody can be wrong all the time, not even the forecasters, and it's not a lot of fun pulling a caravan in the dark, in falling snow and with a two-wheel-drive vehicle. Time enough to eat later. Let me visit Jumbo before I go. The poor old bugger—forgive me, ladies—he'll be wondering where he is and what's adae.'

He had a mutually satisfactory reunion with his still somnolent friend and a minute or two later we heard the van move off.

'That's a stroke of luck,' Isobel said. 'The first one we've had for a while.'

'You can carve that up over the mantelpiece,' I said grimly. 'This is a mess. We're being threatened and the police won't help us because they think that one of us is at the back of it.'

'Count me in with you,' said Charles. 'I seem to be in a similar sort of boat. I don't know whether I can help but I can try.'

'One way . . .' Hannah began. She was looking at me. Under a forthright and sometimes rebellious shell she was a shy girl and rather nervous. 'I'm not suggesting that you do it, not by a mile, but I just think that somebody should point out the possibility. As a last resort, I mean. If you think it would do the trick.'

When she felt unsure of herself, Hannah could go on like that for ever without quite saying anything. 'Point what out?' I asked.

'You could stop all of what's going on, or most of it probably, because we don't really know why Mr Garnet was knocked on the head—'

'How could we stop it?' Beth asked her firmly.

Hannah stopped waffling and came to the point. 'Mr Cunningham could sign the Kennel Club form.'

I was on the point of embarking on an impassioned speech, enumerating the still growing list of events which would have to occur before I would let Ben Garnet profit from his duplicity, but Beth frowned me into silence. 'Can we be sure that that would stop the . . . the persecution?' she asked.

'No,' Henry said, 'we can't be sure. But it seems highly likely. Consider once again the events in sequence. A phone call threatens reprisals if the pups are not legitimized. A man who could very easily be mistaken for John in the dark gets assaulted. The fact that he plays an important role in these events might have been coincidence. But then a dog is poisoned.

'Somebody is trying to force John to sign that form. There you have a neat and compact explanation which embraces all the facts. There may be some other combination, including circumstances which are all unknown to us. But, for the moment, can anybody offer any other explanation which isn't highly improbable and which doesn't entail murderous actions by one of us—which we know to be out of the question?'

The silence which followed was broken by Charles. 'But accepting every point you've made,' he said, 'would anybody really go to such lengths for the sake of a pup's pedigree? Other than Ben Garnet, of course, who has the value of the whole litter at stake and, on present performance, would cheerfully start World War Three to win a bet.'

'Also at stake is his reputation as a master

114

finagler,' Beth said. 'I think that may be as important to him as anything. I can imagine his intimate cronies—the ones who are, if not as twisted as he is, at least trying to catch up—I can just see them having a good chortle with him over his more outrageous coups.'

'Despite all of which, he hardly would or could have knocked himself on the head,' Charles said, completing his original thought.

We others had had more experience than Charles of the lengths of fanaticism to which dog-lovers could sometimes be driven. We looked at Isobel, our expert on breeding lines.

Isobel pushed her spectacles up the bridge of her nose. 'I think it's perfectly possible,' she said. 'Not knocking himself on the head, I don't mean that. But that somebody could become so passionate about it. Both sire and dam are unusually friendly, not to say charming, little dogs, which could create an emotional attachment. But they're also top class both working and trialling—and good looking with it, which is an unusual bonus. They're uncle and niece and their breeding lines mesh together perfectly. You can never be sure—the damnedest traits can pop up from somewhere away in the background—but all the characteristics that one would most like to perpetuate stem from ancestors that they have in common. Frankly, I couldn't have dreamed up a more propitious mating if I'd been asked. It's the kind of breeding a spaniel lover might easily set his heart on and refuse to be turned aside.' Absently, Isobel pushed her hideous spectacles up onto the top of her head and suddenly looked feminine and quite attractive. 'It doesn't only happen about dogs. Once somebody makes up his—or her—mind that "That's what I want and that's what I'm bloody well going to get," the thought either fades out or goes on growing into an obsession.

'And Ben Garnet hadn't missed the point about the breeding. I hear that he was bragging about what he claimed was the inevitable quality of the pups all the time he was haggling with his prospective purchasers. They were going to be world beaters.'

'That's his modus operandi,' Beth said carefully. 'Or one of them. He sets himself a challenge, puts himself in the position of having to make good and then refuses to be turned aside. He starts with flannel, blarney and persuasion, moves on to bluster and then ends up riding roughshod over all opposition if he possibly can. If it's a matter of permission and he can't win out any other way, he just does whatever it is first and apologizes afterwards. Between laying on the charm an inch thick and the reluctance of the average person to get caught up in a lawsuit, he nearly always gets away with it.'

There was a glum little silence as each of us remembered instances when Ben Garnet had 'got away with it.'

'He'll be sorry that he was such an outspoken salesman if he gets a litter throwing back to some hideous ancestor as thick as glue,' Isobel said suddenly. 'But that's beside the point. If we do nothing, or only act defensively, the police aren't going to look in the right directions. What we should do is to take a good look at each of the people who've put their names down for one of the pups.'

'You may be oversimplifying,' said her husband. 'Think a bit more. Suppose Garnet himself sent the threatening message. We're agreed that he didn't knock himself on the head and he was in hospital when the dog was poisoned. We may have Garnet and one or even two of his clients acting in concert or even at cross-purposes.'

'That doesn't change anything,' Beth said. 'Isobel's right. If we start with the clients, but remember what Henry said, I don't see how we can do any harm and we may come up with some facts. Anyway, it'll be better than sitting around on our bums or trying to defend the kennels when the next step may be letter bombs or a whispering campaign.'

'In other words,' I said, 'the best defence is attack?'

'Exactly. But if it's to be done it'll have to be done quickly. In a week's time, Isobel runs Sylvan in the Spaniel Championship, I have to go with her as driver and dosgbody, John's supposed to be handling two dogs in a cocker

117

stake and the weekend's the time that whoever it is is most likely to be free to take the next step in his campaign.'

We all roused. There was a stirring of the Dunkirk spirit until Daffy spoiled it. 'But who are these clients?' she asked.

The Dunkirk spirit began to wither.

'Seven pups,' Charles said. 'That's according to Mrs Garnet. And I understand that they're all spoken for.'

'That makes seven suspects,' Henry said. 'Eight if you include Garnet himself as the possible originator of the phone call. Don't we know any of them?'

There was no immediate response.

'I don't think we do,' said Isobel at last. 'And I don't see Ben Garnet handing out a list.'

'I think I can tell you one of them,' Charles said. 'My architect, Lewis Sowerby. I met him with the builder on site when the job was starting. The builder mentioned that there were spaniel pups on the way. He went over to talk with Garnet and came back looking tickled pink.'

'That makes sense,' I said. 'Unfortunately, I can't ask him about it. Lewis Sowerby masterminded our conversion work here and I sold him a puppy. Just recently, the poor bitch was accidentally shot—not by Sowerby, to be fair to him, but by a Belgian visitor, a client of his, who got over-excited. The Belgian coughed up the price of a fully trained replacement and

118

Sowerby trotted round here expecting me to welcome him and his Belgian francs. By that time, I'd decided that he wasn't a fit person to own a dog and I told him to go and bowl his hoop.'

'Why was that?' Daffy asked curiously.

'A long story,' I said. 'I'll tell you in strict confidence some time when we're not so quite so fraught.'

'I'll have a word with Lewis on Monday,' Charles said, 'without telling him who wants to know, and see what I can find out. He may even know some of the other purchasers.'

Beth was looking concerned. 'I quite see that you can't ring him up during the weekend to be nosy about his purchase of somebody else's pup,' she said, 'but won't you be back in London on Monday? This isn't the kind of chat you can have over the phone without starting somebody wondering.'

'Didn't I tell you?' said Charles. 'I've finished in London and I don't start the new job for a fortnight. For the moment, I'm a gentleman of leisure apart from settling any outstanding details about the new house and planning the garden. My wife's still in London, seeing to the storage of our chattels pending completion of the house here. She'll be joining me in a week's time and we'll move to a small private hotel for several months. I can be around to give you any help you want.'

It seemed to me that we could use all the

help we could get. Even an extra pair of eyes to watch out for vandals and saboteurs would free one of the firm for other urgent duties. I was on the point of offering him the use of our spare bedroom when a glare from Beth stopped me.

Often, Beth and I each know what the other is about to say. Close contact even over the few years of our marriage has led to an understanding of how each other's mind works. More than that; I believe that actual telepathy often develops between husbands and wives. My reaction to this unconventional form of communication is to let it save me the bother of verbalizing; Beth speaks out anyway. As a consequence, one of our few areas of dissent is that I consider her a chatterbox while she sometimes thinks me close-tongued; but since this is a common bone of contention between husband and wife we never let it worry us.

This time, I knew exactly what Beth wanted to say. I liked Charles. As well as being a good client—there are not many who would consider buying two pups in successive weeks—he was an open and likeable man. As a result I had closed my mind to the fact that he had as good a motive as anybody, and better than most, for whacking Ben Garnet over his head. If he had done so, I thought, I for one would have treated him to no more than a click of the tongue and a mildly reproving headshake. But it was in theory conceivable that the threatening message and the poisoning of his own dog had followed in an attempt to camouflage what might well be considered an attempt at murder.

Beth got to her feet and began gathering dirty dishes. 'When did you come up from London?' she asked casually.

The question might have been no more than a polite follow-up to his own statement. I sensed that Charles quite understood its implications, but he replied with equal courtesy. 'My colleagues gave a farewell party for me at lunchtime yesterday. After that I was free. I left the car with my wife and flew up. I'd booked a hire car and it was waiting for me at Turnhouse Airport.'

Too many questions would certainly both warn and alienate him. 'See what you can get out of Sowerby,' I told him. 'In particular, whether he knows of any other purchasers. Meantime, somebody had better go and see Mrs Garnet.'

'You,' Beth said.

'She'd listen to a woman,' I suggested.

Beth shook her head. 'That's not her reputation.'

'All the more reason.'

'Think of yourself,' she said, quite straight-faced, 'as a human sacrifice on the altar of our solvency; and don't part with your virtue until you've got the whole list or I'll be furious.'

Beth sometimes gets a rush of frivolity to the head. This time, I decided to ignore it.

'Henry—?' I began.

'My days as a lady-charmer are behind me.'

'Very, very far indeed,' said Isobel absently.

'And I can hardly approach her again,' said Charles. He had got up to help Beth and was busily stacking crockery in the dishwasher. 'She thinks I'm trying to back out of a deal because her husband's in hospital. It seems to be down to you.'

'All right,' I said wearily. 'I'll go tomorrow morning. Who else? Who's that man who turns up on Crail's shoots? I think he has a garage but I can't remember where. He's secretary of the syndicate where Ben Garnet's a member and, I gathered, not a very popular one.'

'I've got to be going,' Daffy said. 'Rex is at home and he'll be wanting his little comforts. The man you want is Mr Cochrane and he has the garage and filling station at Muircraigs.'

Hannah got up with her. 'I'll go and give the pups their last feed,' she said, 'and make sure the dogs are all settled.'

'They'll soon get unsettled when Joe and his brother turn up,' I told her, 'but by all means feed the pups as soon as one of us is ready to come with you. I don't want you out there on your own after dark.'

'And I don't want to keep the pups waiting,' Hannah retorted. 'If I scream, you'll hear me over that thing.' She nodded towards the loudspeaker which at that moment was relaying the sound of a dog chasing rabbits in its sleep.

'I'd be happier if there was somebody outside,' Beth said gently. 'The dogs might not bark at an intruder if they happened to know him.'

I was preparing to give in gracefully to both of them by escorting Hannah about her duties when Joe's van was heard approaching, labouring with the effort of pulling a caravan which turned out to be not only large but, being slightly dated, also heavy.

We all turned out, including Sam, to supervise the placement of the caravan. The kennels and their accompanying runs are arranged in squares of four along both sides of a central path. To permit the occasional access of vehicles, the path was broad and finished in tarmac; but it would not have been wide enough for Joe's van to be extracted if it had pulled the caravan into a position strategically central to the kennels and within view of the house.

So it was all hands to push and then to shake the hand of Joe's half-brother Dave. I ran out an electricity cable for them and showed them where to draw water. Beth told them to make use of the facilities in the house during waking hours.

'You're sure you'll be all right here?' Beth asked anxiously.

'This is luxury after yon field,' Dave said. He was the image of Joe but smaller and a few years older. 'Tarmac underfoot, electricity laid on and the water only a few yards away. You'll have a job getting rid of us when the time comes.' I thought to myself that it was not the stance of the caravan which might detain them. Dave seemed to have taken a fancy to Hannah.

After that it was necessary to adjust the sensors on the floodlights and warn them to watch their language when within earshot of the microphones. By then, the new arrivals had been accepted and when I reached the house again I could hear that the dogs were settling down to sleep.

We got to bed at last. I was tired enough to sleep, despite all the worries which were chasing each other's tails through my mind like overactive puppies.

CHAPTER SIX

Although I seemed to sleep like the dead my mind must have been at work, because I awoke with my thoughts, which had been in a tangle when I went to bed, now tidily arranged for as far ahead as reasoning could carry them. Not very far, as it turned out. There had been no alarms in the night, the dogs were all safe and sound and a careful search uncovered no poisoned meat lying near the runs. The caravan looked as though it had always been part of the scene.

I made sure that the answering function of the telephone remained switched off. Any further threatening messages would have to be delivered personally. But I also fetched my radio cassette recorder and attached it to the static part of the cordless phone in the kitchen where, rather to my surprise, it worked perfectly well; and when the girls joined us for breakfast and Isobel arrived from her home, I made sure that everybody knew how to operate it and I expounded on the ghastly fate reserved for anybody who failed to tape any incoming calls, at least until they had proved to be irrelevant. As usual, the ladies nodded and smiled and went their own ways, but I hoped that the message had got through.

Dogs do not recognize the Sabbath and Sunday is often the only day on which a man is free to come in search of a new Best Friend. Much of the firm's work has to continue and very often Sunday receives only token acknowledgement. I had been hoping to spend the day and much of the succeeding week putting a polish on the dogs entered for the following weekend's competitions, but now it seemed to be generally agreed that I would have to spend my time spearheading our investigations.

Isobel, after looking in on Jumbo, who was now fully restored to consciousness and fretting for his beloved owner, had intended to devote herself to her records and the firm's accounts, but I persuaded her to let the paperwork slide and take over the bulk of my training duties.

Joe looked in. I decided that one has to start by trusting somebody. So far, he knew about the poisoning and the assault on Ben Garnet. When I told him about the threatening message and the theory that Garnet had been attacked in mistake for me, he looked genuinely shocked. 'I'll stay off work and help if I can,' he said immediately. 'I said I'd go in and peg out the drain tracks today, ready for the JCB the morn, but I've done enough to let him get started.'

'Go and earn some extra daily bread,' I told him. 'But ask Dave to keep an eye on the place. Somebody seems determined that the breeding of those pups should be authenticated but if we caved in it would mean letting him get away with murdering poor Accer. Anyway, we're damned if we're going to be ripped off that way. We'll be trying to find out who the purchasers are. I'll be visiting Mrs Garnet but, if you happen to see her, you might get more out of the lady than I could.'

'I'll try,' he said. 'I'm not hopeful.'

'I thought you said she was a nice-like body.'

'Aye. She is that, though it wasna' me as said it. But she took to coming across the park and trying to tell the digger-driver where to dump his spoil and when not to fash her with the blatter of his engine. In the end, I had to tell her that we took orders from Mr McArthur and she'd best speak to him.'

After a moment's thought he added, 'I can tell you one of the purchasers and that's my boss, Mr McArthur himself. But he's not the kind to be up to anything of that sort. Mr Garnet pressured him into taking a pup. He was happy enough with the deal but not so keen that he'd go overboard about it. Anyway, it was a bitch he wanted and he was going to have her spayed after her first season, so he wouldn't be fashing hisself over registration and a pedigree. He just wants a dog to train up for the shoot he belongs to over in Angus. What's more, he was in Glasgow yesterday.'

'Is there a Mrs McArthur?'

'Aye, there is.' Joe grinned suddenly. 'But she was saying that she's not having a damned dog in the house and that if a dog comes in the boss goes out, so Mr McArthur's got two of the lads building a kennel and run in the garden this minute, copying them off the drawings of the ones we did for you.'

That seemed to account for one purchaser and his wife, subject to confirmation. 'Will you see what other names you can get?' I asked.

'Well, I'll try,' Joe said. 'But I'm dashed if I see how.'

I prepared to settle down at the phone. Beth, ever the opportunist, persuaded me into one of the basket chairs in the kitchen so that I could supervise Sam and let her get on with the household chores and then do some gardening.

Beth takes the business very seriously, but her real emotional attachment is to the house and the garden—and, of course, the dogs themselves.

My first call was to Ben Garnet's number but I came up on an answering machine. Either Mrs Garnet was already out hospital visiting or else she was still in bed. I hung up.

I had more luck with Mr Cochrane at the Muircraigs Garage and Filling Station. His voice answered the phone and he recognized my name when I identified myself.

'Have I caught you at a good moment?' I asked him.

'The best,' he said chuckling. 'The laddie's manning the pumps. This is my day for doing the accounts and the VAT and, truth is, I've had mair nor enough for the moment. Let me get my pipe going and I'll news awa' wi' you till the cows come home.' I heard a match strike and a puffing sound. 'So,' he said. 'What's adae?'

'It's about your syndicate member, Ben Garnet,' I said.

'What's the bugger done now? Whatever it is,' Cochrane added cautiously, 'he'd no authority to commit the shoot to anything.' His tone suggested that he had had more than enough of Mr Garnet. 'Anything he's been up to's on his own head. And that includes being dunted on it. You heard about that?'

'It happened on my doorstep, more or less,' I told him. 'You remember when my dog

128

coupled with his bitch?'

'At Lord Crail's shoot. Aye, I mind it fine. I'd no doubt it was done a-purpose. I'd been thinking that the canny bugger would serve the bitch hissel' rather than pay a stud fee. But I couldna' swear to it, if that's what you're after.'

'Nothing like that. There's seven pups, I'm told, and I wondered if you could put me in touch with any of the purchasers.'

'I can put you on to twa o' them,' he said.

'You can?'

'Aye. They're members o' the shoot. Yon mannie Garnet can be a pain in the arse, whiles, but that's a damn good wee bitch he has—otherwise we wouldna' thole him. We missed her sair when she was o'er far on to be worked. And then he was bragging that the pups should be as good as the dam or even better, because of the line-breeding. We're short of dogs on our shoot—some of the members could keep a dog but haven't the time or the skill to train a pup.'

'They could buy a trained dog,' I pointed out hopefully.

'And a Purdey for Sunday best,' Cochrane retorted, seemingly forgetting that Sunday shooting of live quarry is frowned on in Scotland. 'But Jamie Kinglass, who's a rare hand with a dog, he said he'd take one and if any other member did the same he'd keep the pup for him and train them both on as long as he was paid for the cost of the feed, no mair'n

129

that. There was one taker. Then another lad made up his mind to take on a pup but Ben said that they was a' spoken for by then. Point is, yon was a bargain you couldna' match.'

'I wouldn't try,' I said. I thought for a few seconds, wondering how to get what I wanted without spreading the news all round the east of Scotland, which gave him time to relight his pipe. I heard the match again and the puffing.

'Were you shooting yesterday?' I asked.

'Yestreen? No. We've about shot the ground out of last year's releases, those that hadna' strayed off or been taken by foxes and hawks,' he said. Before I could get my hopes up he went on, 'We had a working party instead, checking snares and making ready. We're planning to start wi' day-olds this year.'

'Good turnout?'

'A'body except Ben Garnet. And we couldna' blame him for that, him being in Ninewells. We slogged awa' until the pub opened but we got the most of it done.'

Stoutly resisting the temptation to chat about their plans for keepering, I got the names of the other pup buyers and, after an exchange of courtesies, rang off.

*   *   *

Sam was determined to imitate one of the helicopters from Leuchars, which were frequent overhead visitors and very annoying to humans. The dogs soon learned to ignore them. Sam's noise was even more shattering than the real thing. I managed to settle him down at last with the only quiet toy that he would ever tolerate, a complicated set of building blocks that I had never taken the time to figure out although Sam enjoyed solving the geometric problems.

There had been something familiar about the recorded message on Ben Garnet's answering machine. I keyed the number again, but this time, when I wanted the answering machine, Mrs Garnet answered. We keep early hours at the kennels, even on a Sunday, and I decided that she had probably been sleeping when I made the first call. It had been far too early for hospital visiting.

'This is John Cunningham,' I said.

'Ah yes. The father of Cleo's pups.'

'Yes. Not personally, you understand,' I paused, but the comment seemed to pass her by. 'Could I drive over and see you for a minute? I could be with you in a quarter of an hour. I wouldn't need much of your time.'

'Is it to bring me the Kennel Club form? Ben said that you might come with it.'

I wondered which of them was living in a dream-world. Garnet, as Beth had observed, was inclined to give to the world as fact his version of whatever he wanted to happen, perhaps as an incentive to himself to move mountains and make it come true. I had met

Mrs Garnet once, briefly, and I could picture her, a slightly faded but still pretty woman with a provocative body below an innocent face. From what I had heard as well as from my own observation, she was either unaware of her husband's reputation and of his misdeeds or else she had a remarkable acting ability. As always, the truth, I thought, would lie somewhere in between—that she could or would not accept what she knew and therefore rejected it. I never decided whether to despise her blindness or admire her loyalty.

'Not exactly,' I said. 'Can I come over and explain?'

'It's not very convenient,' she said firmly. 'Ben wants me to do a host of errands for him before I go in to visit.'

In the face of that allusion I could hardly not ask after him. 'How is he mending?' I asked.

She became more forthcoming. 'They're very pleased with him. His scan came up clear. The concussion's passing off and he's got most of his memory back. I'll probably have him home again in a day or two. Apparently he has a very thick skull.'

Well, I could have told her that. 'Excellent,' I said, keeping the disappointment out of my voice. 'About coming to see you . . ?'

'What is it,' she asked impatiently, 'that's so serious that we can't settle over the phone?'

Rather than emphasize the seriousness by arguing, I gave in with apparent casualness. If I blew it, I blew it. 'It's about that Kennel Club form. There are one or two people around who shouldn't be allowed to own a dog—'

For once I seemed to have struck a sympathetic nerve. 'That's very true,' she said with feeling. 'It's owners who should be licensed, not dogs. Something with a test to pass, like a driving licence, that can be taken away.'

This was a subject on which I was in strong agreement but I refused to be drawn. 'So before I consider signing the form I want to know who his purchasers are.'

I waited, almost holding my breath.

'I quite understand,' she said. 'And you're so right. I wish I could help you. But Ben dealt with all that. The only one I know of is Sheila Campsie. She came to see me, wanting me to drive for Meals on Wheels, but Ben likes to have me around to act as his secretary at a moment's notice. Anyway, it was just after the pups were born and she fell in love with them. I'm sure she'll be a good owner. She'd be more likely to kill with kindness than any other way. I can ask Ben about the others when I see him, if you like.'

'Please do,' I said. That should give Ben Garnet something to think about. With a little luck it might see him on the way to a relapse.

'I must go now. Please sign that form, Mr Cunningham. Ben will be so disappointed if you don't. I'm sure that the worry of it is setting back his recovery. Goodbye.'

She rang off, leaving me feeling slightly out of focus.

The house was, for once, empty apart from Sam and myself. I needed to talk to the others, in particular Beth who I could see pruning the early roses. And it would be an excuse to leave Sam outside. I fitted him into his outdoor woollies to his loudly expressed displeasure. Like officer Gribble, he seemed not to feel the cold.

Outside, the sun was blinding at first and surprisingly warm although it was only thawing the surface of the ground and leaving it ready to freeze again into a skating rink. I popped Sam into his special enclosure. It was almost impossible to keep the grass perpetually clean. Sam had seen the puppies sniffing at dog turds and believed that what was all right for the dogs was all right for him; but we had fenced off his own patch of lawn. Dogs lived one side, Sam could run free the other, and never the twain should meet except under adult supervision. He ignored the pedal-car that had cost me the selling price of a good pup and made straight for his favourite toy—a plastic milk bottle on a length of string.

'Who,' I asked Beth, 'is Sheila Campsie?'

She tried to look up at me, shook her head and made an extraordinary face as she tried, apparently, to blow up her own nose. I pushed back the offending lock of her hair for her.

'Thanks. Mrs Campsie,' she said absently. 'Oh, you know her.'

'I do?'

'Well, you've certainly seen her. She's off her rocker. Help me up. The rest of the roses haven't yet budded enough to be pruneable. I've started too early, really, but the mild autumn brought some of them on and we're always so busy just at the time the garden needs attention.'

I pulled her to her feet. 'When have I seen Mrs Campsie?' I asked patiently.

'Oh, you know. She's that woman who's always protesting about something. Those were her and her daughter outside the gates at Freddy Crail's shoot. She lives just outside Cupar. Her husband left her plenty of money and not enough to do.' Beth took off her thick gloves and picked up her bag of prunings. 'I'll sand the paths again before I come in. You'd better get back inside before you freeze. Take Sam with you.'

'In a minute,' I said. 'If Mrs Campsie's anti-shooting, what does she want with a spaniel of working strain? According to Mrs Garnet, she's one of the purchasers.'

'She's mad about dogs but she thinks that working them is cruel. Somebody told me that she has a whole pack of Labs and spaniels and GSPs, all in the house and all over the furniture. She probably thinks that she's saving them from an awful fate. I told you, she's off

135

her rocker. Now will you get back indoors and take Sam with you?'

I collected Sam from his private lawn. 'I thought I'd got rid of you for a bit,' I told him.

Sam was at the age for overhearing and repeating the conversation of the grown-ups, especially those parts which would least bear repetition. 'Mrs Campsie's off her rocker,' he shouted and let loose a burst of maniacal laughter while cocking an eye to observe my reaction. I kept a poker face and lifted him out of his corral. With a bit of luck he would soon forget that nugget of acquired wisdom.

Before we got as far as the front door a car came rolling up the drive. With the alarms and excursions of the last few days fresh in my mind, I was ready to dive for cover taking Sam with me—the habits drilled into you by a military career tend to linger on—but the big Volvo only disgorged a young couple in search of a pup.

They knew what they wanted and were sure that they had found it in the sole remaining member of the last but one litter. First, quite rightly, they wanted to see the dam put through her paces. I was fizzing with impatience to get on with the next phase of my enquiries, but there would be no point in averting a threat to the business while letting the business go to pot. They made no objection to Sam accompanying us into the field although they did blink when he repeated his newfound opinion of Mrs Campsie.

After Moonbeam had faithfully demonstrated her talents, the couple took the puppy away with them, leaving behind a satisfactory cheque. He would, the man said, bring her back for training when time and the pup were ripe.

It was rather more than an hour well spent and it had used up a part of the day which might otherwise have been largely wasted. When I looked at my watch, the morning was advanced. By now, Mrs Garnet might well have left for Dundee to visit the injured.

I took Sam back into the warm kitchen with me and stripped off our outermost layers. Soup was already simmering on the cooker. Prepared to hang up instantly if the Garnets' phone rang more than four times, I was gratified when the answering machine cut in after only two rings, indicating that there was a message waiting.

As I had supposed, the recorded voice was familiar. One can put a message in one's own voice on a tapeless answering machine, but the message is lost at the first power cut or whenever the phone is moved to a different socket. The system then reverts to the original, standard recording. The average subscriber eventually tires of redictating the message.

There is a facility for listening to one's messages from another phone but on the simpler machines there is no protection by code to stop any Nosy Parker from making use of the same facility. I waited for the end of the long beep, pressed the noughts and crosses symbol for a count of four and then listened. A voice, gruff but without much accent, said, 'This is Jamie. Have you got that pedigree fixed up yet? I'm not taking the pup without it. Let me know quickly—I've been offered another working pup. See you.'

I hung up. I could have erased the message but there seemed to be no point. It might even have called to her attention the fact that an outsider was intercepting her messages. Then, if she dialled 1471, she would even be given my number as having been the originator of the last call. I thought that I had no way of knowing whether Mrs Garnet had already listened to the message. Either way, the next incoming call would erase it. It would be interesting to see whether she told me about 'Jamie'.

Sam had installed himself in the other basket chair and had whiled away the time imitating my every move. Phones had begun to fascinate him. The wall mounting for the cordless phone in the kitchen was just coming within his reach. He was never allowed into the sitting room unsupervised, but one had to be very careful not to leave the phone within his reach. I put the cordless phone on the high shelf where it now spent most of the daytime hours.

When Beth came into the room and began laying out the ingredients for our midday snack—too light and informal to be dignified

138

with the title of 'lunch'—Sam ran to her. Food was more fascinating even than telephones. Beth picked him up and dumped him firmly on my knee where he squirmed for a few seconds and then settled down.

'Keep him in one place for a few seconds,' Beth said.

'Will do. Tell me more about Mrs Campsie.' I hushed Sam quickly before he could get started again.

'I think I've told you all I know,' she said. 'The others will be here in a minute. Ask them.'

'Is Henry coming?' In times of difficulty or doubt, he was the first I would turn to for advice or knowledge of the world.

'Henry's gone up to Aberdeen. Joe's knocked off for the day. I told him to join us. Dave can stand guard and Joe can take him out some food later.'

Sure enough, as though drawn by the smell of food, Isobel came in. Sylvan, she said, had almost forgotten her manners and had been on the point of chasing a rabbit; but she had come to her senses almost instantly and would not, Isobel thought, have been penalized by even the strictest judge. Hannah arrived seconds later and set to washing the grime of her morning's labours off at the sink. Daffy, who was supposed to be on a day off, came in to hear any news that was going and took a place at the table anyway. She looked more outrageous than ever, the pink stripe in her hair clashing abominably with the turquoise of what I could only think of as a tabard.

Joe and Charles came in last. 'I chapped on Mrs Garnet's door but she wasn't at home,' Joe said.

'She'll be off to Ninewells,' Beth said, putting out mugs of soup. She included Charles, who had come with Joe from the site of his house, and he accepted her hospitality with only a token hesitation.

'I caught her on the phone,' I said. 'She tells me that one of the pups is earmarked for Mrs Campsie.'

'She's off her rocker,' Sam announced loudly before I could stop him.

Everybody laughed and Daffy said, 'If he means Mrs Campsie, he's not wrong.'

'Don't encourage him,' I told them. 'He could say that in the wrong company and start a feud. Or a lawsuit. Beth says that she's ... mildly eccentric, pro-animal and anti-sport, a protester. Well, anyone's entitled to be wrong if that's what turns them on. Can anybody tell me any more about the lady?'

Sam stirred in his chair. 'Not you,' I told him.

Daffy can be counted on to know all about everybody. 'She lives on the back road out of Cupar heading this way, four or five miles from the town. Big, newish house that looks as though it belongs in the middle of a suburb, not out in the backwoods—God alone knows how they got planning permission. She's also antinuclear, Greenham Common and all that jazz. She doesn't only protest about things, she's very much into good works—'

'Meals on Wheels,' I put in.

'That's right. And she's a voluntary helper with all sorts of charitable bodies. She was sorely missed when she got herself sent down for ten days.'

'She's been in the pokey?'

'Didn't you know? It was all over the local rag. She sprayed a policeman with paint during a Ban the Atom demo,' Daffy said. 'And then she refused to pay for the damage to his uniform. Otherwise, she'd have got off.'

'She doesn't seem to be the sort of person to buy a gun-dog pup,' Hannah observed. 'I mean, she'd melt into a group of our usual clients like . . . like a cat in a flock of pigeons.'

'More like a pigeon,' Joe said, 'in a . . . a what of cats?'

'I don't think there is a collective noun for cats,' said Charles. 'The cat's too solitary an animal.'

'Let's try to stick to one subject,' I said. Such was the nature of mealtime chats at Three Oaks that we might easily have spent the next half hour inventing ever unlikelier collective nouns.

'Really, she doesn't seem to be the sort of person to do any of the things she does,' Beth remarked. 'That's pretty much what John said. She seems so dull and respectable. Her trouble is that she has a whole lot of bees in rather a lot of bonnets. It's a pity, really, because she's a nice person underneath it all. I think she just adores dogs indiscriminately and pays no heed to what they were bred for.'

Joe swallowed a large mouthful whole. 'Church on Sunday in gloves and her best hat. I think she only goes to pray for the birds and bunnies. She has a daughter living with her,' he said.

Daffy stared at him. 'Joe's blushing,' she said. 'Are you sweet on the daughter, Joe?'

If Joe had not been blushing before he definitely was now. 'She's a bit above my touch,' he said. 'Her mum looks at me as though I'm a piece of sh . . . sharn,' he amended hastily, 'just because I work with my hands. But I've fetched her home from the hops a time or two and we get on great. She's a wee cracker,' he finished.

Joe was no longer a manual worker but a valued member of the building team, but this was neither the time nor the company in which to pursue details of Joe's amours although I could see Beth making up her mind to pursue her own enquiries next time that she had Joe to herself.

'Getting back to the mother,' I said firmly, '—although I'm sure the daughter's much more interesting—Mrs C seems to be a fanatic, but could she be enough of a fanatic, either about the pup or about field sports, to want to assault

142

me and poison a dog?'

'She'd be more like to poison me,' Joe said. 'Mind you, June, the daughter, would never get mixed up in anything bad.'

'She was carrying a placard along with her mother on the day of Lord Crail's shoot,' I said.

'Aye. She does that to oblige her mum,' Joe said. 'But she doesn't mean a word of it. She used to go beagling when she was a student, she told me, and she'd be beagling yet if it wasn't for that mother of hers. She sneaks out to help out as a beater, once in a while. The other beaters never let on, if they see her carrying a board with her mother the next week.'

That seemed to exhaust the subject of Mrs Campsie. 'I'll find an excuse to go and see the lady,' I said. 'And now to the next item of business.' I wiped honey off my fingers and got up to play the tape that I had made of the message stolen from the Garnets' answering machine. 'Would anybody care to put a name to that voice?'

'I've heard it,' Isobel said after a long hiatus. 'Or one very like it. Not often and not recently and I'm damned if I can remember when or where. Leave the tape where I can play it over now and again and maybe it'll come to me. And I'll play it to Henry.'

'No other offers?' I asked. 'Then that's how we'll have to leave it for the moment. All we know about him is his voice.'

'We know more than that,' Hannah said

softly.

'You know him?' Beth said.

Hannah shook her head. 'I didn't say that. I know something about him. And so do you. For a start, we know that he doesn't know that Mr Garnet's in hospital.'

'We don't know how old the message is,' said Daffy. 'It could have been on the machine since before Mr Garnet got whacked.'

Joe made a negative sound in his throat. 'Mr McArthur left a message on her machine for Mrs Garnet yesterday, just something polite to say that he hoped her husband would be home soon. This has to be after that.'

'Right,' Hannah said. 'And he's insisting on the pup being registered, so he wants to breed or to compete.'

'Or maybe to show,' Beth said, 'though our breeding isn't for showing. We breed for health and working ability and we like the looks that come as a result, and never mind what the Kennel Club says a spaniel should look like. He may just be keeping his options open in case the pup turns out well.'

'Could be,' I said. 'Anything else?'

'There's a trace of an accent,' Hannah said.

I played the tape again. Although the telephone usually exaggerates an accent, this one was very faint. I still thought American, Daffy thought Belfast and Isobel was sure that it was Australian. Or possibly New Zealand, she added.

'Let's do some figuring,' I said. 'There are seven pups; one earmarked for Mrs Campsie, two for members of the shoot run by Mr Cochrane, one for Charles's architect, one for Joe's boss. That's five. Plus two we don't know about. Yet.'

'I don't want to cause another digression,' Charles said, 'but I still don't know why you wouldn't sell Lewis Sowerby a puppy.'

'I just don't think he's a fit owner.'

'Oh come on,' Daffy said. 'We won't give you any peace until you've coughed up the story.'

'And if there's anything wrong with the man who designed my house,' Charles said, 'I want to know about it.'

I gave an ostentatious sigh, just to let them know that I was plagued by nosy people with butterfly minds. 'He's a gadget fiend,' I said. 'His answer to any of life's problems is to buy or make some complicated device to do the job for him. He bought a young dog from me a few years ago. He was fixated on the dog but he'd built himself a new house in Broughty Ferry, a bit of a show house by all accounts and fitted with everything that opens and shuts, and his wife was fixated on the house. Any time the dog went out into the garden to do his business and came in again she swore that she could smell the doings on him. It got so that she didn't want the dog in the house at all.

'So, Sowerby being what he is, instead of building an outside kennel like any sensible man, he almost rebuilt the utility room where the dog slept. He made a short tunnel under the fitments with a flap at each end and a delay so that the dog couldn't walk straight through. And he put in a spray of warm, soapy water where the dog's back end would be, followed by fresh water followed by hot air. This only switched on when the dog was inward bound, you understand.'

'Sounds like a good idea,' Beth said. She sounded at least half serious. 'We could do with something like that.'

'If we go for it,' I said, 'we won't let Sowerby design it. At the first shot, it lifted the poor beast clean off the floor and more or less pinned it to the overhead surface.'

'Like a ping-pong ball at a shooting gallery?' Hannah suggested.

'Exactly like. The poor tyke had a terror of dog-flaps after that and Sowerby brought it to me, asking me to train the dog to use his contraption after he'd de-tuned it. I told him he was out of his skull. We were still arguing about it when the dog was killed a couple of months later. That's why I won't sell him another pup. God alone knows what high-tech idiocies he'd inflict on it. Can we get on, now?'

'Fire ahead,' Beth said.

'Of the last two pups,' I said, 'one may go to the man on the tape. But as Hannah pointed out, it doesn't seem that he knows that Garnet's in hospital, in which case he couldn't

146

have put him there. Unless it's a bluff for the benefit of the police. Either way, we want to know who he is.'

'Finally, there's one more. We believe that they're all spoken for but, if that's true, we know nothing about the last one.'

'We'll ask around,' Daffy said. Somebody must know. Now, while I'm here, are you coping?' she asked Hannah.

The two girls got up and began preparing feeds. Charles said that he would go along with them—to lend a hand, he said, but when he borrowed a pair of dummies I knew that he intended to visit Sid.

The gathering broke up. I moved to the basket chair and looked up Mrs Campsie's number.

My first call to Mrs Campsie was unanswered—not even by an answering machine which might have coughed up some fragment of information. Just a distant unceasing ring which told me nothing except that nobody picked up the call.

The girls were ready with feed; suitable diets for young pups and the nursing dam, and a diet high in protein and calcium for the one pregnant boarder. Beth gave Charles a tray with a plate and mug. 'Give it to Dave, if he's still on guard,' she said.

'And if he isn't, come back and tell me,' I put in. 'This isn't a good day for being sneaked up on.' In retrospect, it wasn't my day for syntax either.

Isobel had gone out to resume her work on Sylvan after exacting a promise from me to join her later, to throw dummies and fire blanks for her.

I tried Mrs Campsie's number again with no better result.

Beth was finishing her own lunch which had, as usual, been delayed by the needs of Sam. I got out of my chair and began the washing-up by hand. 'Who do we know,' I asked over my shoulder, 'who knows Mrs Garnet well enough to ask her whose voice that is?'

'I can think of one or two. But how would they explain having heard a message from the Garnets' answering machine? It's probably covered by the Data Protection Act or something.'

I chewed on that one while drying the dishes but, although I was fairly sure that the law had not yet taken account of answering machines, there was no obvious answer. I did however come up with one fresh thought. The news of the assault on Ben Garnet had made the local papers but not until after the message might already have been left on Garnet's answering machine. The gruff-voiced man might still have been responsible for the attack, the threatening message and the poisoning if he was under the impression that I was the man he had struck down. In which case, if I were the real target, he would by now have realized his mistake.

Ouch!

I seemed to be stymied for the moment. On the principle of *when in doubt do something useful,* I decided to spare Isobel a few minutes to take the two cockers onto the Moss in preparation for Saturday's trial. There would be little on offer but rabbits, but a dog which is steady to fur can be steady to anything. A fox had managed to dig into our rabbit pen and although the slaughter had been minimal any survivors had escaped through the tunnel which the fox had dug for them. I would borrow a ferret and some purse-nets and restock the pen when I had time to spare, if that day ever dawned.

My good intentions went for nothing. I was still gathering up what I needed when the portly figure of Constable Buchan arrived at the door.

Buchan was unusually friendly and considerate. He asked politely whether he might come in. I took him into the sitting room and put a match to the fire.

'Captain—' he began and then corrected himself. 'Mr Cunningham, I'm sent by Inspector Burrard to get a statement from you. I'm sorry.'

'That's all right,' I said. 'Normal procedure.' I might well have asked him why he was so apologetic about obtaining a statement, but I could make a good guess. If the Inspector had believed that I had been the intended victim of

149

the assault and that the threatening message was genuine, he would not have left the next interview to the local Bobby. All that he was hoping for would be that I would commit myself to what he still believed to be the lies I had already told him, to be used against me once he had evidence.

We had to go slowly because Buchan was writing down my answers in longhand as well as making notes on a typed document which I took to be a transcript from the tapes of my earlier dealings with the Inspector. For once, I tried to be a model of patience. I explained Beth's belief that I had left the house on Thursday evening. 'I still think that she's mistaken,' I said, 'but she could be right. Such a stroll wouldn't be routine or significant—one of the girls usually does the last round, to check on the dogs and take a feed to any newly weaned pups; mine would just be for a breath of air while I ordered my thoughts. Not the kind of thing you remember to put in your diary.'

'I understand,' he said. He wrote it all down. We spent a full half-hour on our working routine as affecting a potential poisoner.

'I think that's the lot,' he said at last.

'Satisfied?' I said.

It was a casual remark rather than a serious question but I saw his face darken. 'In a way I'm satisfied. Between ourselves—?' (I nodded) '—I'm satisfied that you're telling the

150

absolute truth. We've had dealings before and what I know of you bears out what you're telling me. Aye, and what I know about Mr Garnet as well. The Inspector only knows the facts he's been told about and he doesn't know the folks at all.'

Whatever iniquities were being practised on me they were no fault of Buchan's, but I decided that I might as well ram the message home in the hope of enlisting sympathy or support. 'So although I've been threatened and one of my dogs was poisoned,' I said, 'and a man who looks very like me was attacked near here in the dark, the police aren't going to look out for me?'

'My orders are to keep any eye on the place,' Buchan said.

'Between your other duties?'

'Aye.' Buchan lifted his chin and looked stubborn. 'But that's not to say that I'd turn my back on you. I've a duty to guard against crime, whether or no some Inspector tells me to. I took a good look round late last night and again early the morn and twice more since. More nor that I can't manage.'

'Thank you for that much,' I said. I was touched by his concern but I had a concern of my own. If he had visited late at night, the Constable must have been lucky not to have been pounced on by Joe or Dave. If several men were going to guard independently, they had better know about each other. On the

151

other hand, an immediate visit to the caravan might not be a good idea. Rather than risk Dave becoming over-enthusiastic with a shotgun, I had lent him my Conservator dart-gun—a necessary item of equipment at a quarantine kennels, but one which I had on a previous occasion had cause to use on a human being and had found remarkably effective.

The dart-gun might have the advantage of leaving very little mark and no other evidence once the victim had recovered, but Buchan might not be impressed to find Joe's brother-in-law sitting outside the caravan with something resembling a rifle or shotgun across his knees like some old-time sheriff in a bad Western. 'Friends of ours are staying in their caravan right among the kennels,' I said, 'so between you and them we should be safe. If you come into the grounds at night, you'd better be ready to identify yourself to them— quickly, just in case they mistake you for an intruder of evil intent.'

Buchan looked uncertain whether to be relieved or offended that we should have taken precautions of our own without relying on our wonderful police. When he had taken himself off, I hurried down to the caravan. As I supposed, Dave, well wrapped up against the day, was pacing around the kennels with the dart-gun at the ready. I warned him that policemen as well as poisoners might be on the prowl.

CHAPTER SEVEN

Charles intercepted me on my way back to the house. He had Sid with him, walking tight to heel. When we stopped, the dog sat. I noticed that Sid was already eyeing Charles with the devotion that a spaniel can show to a master but usually reserves for the customary provider of food. Charles's manner was definitely proprietorial.

'The dragon-lady made me go and help her,' he said plaintively. 'I've only just got around to having another session with Hob.'

I hid my smile. If the name-change was already in use then Charles had made up his mind, whether he knew it or not.

'Isobel isn't a dragon,' I said. 'She's a very gentle soul. Sometimes she forgets that she isn't still talking to spaniels, that's all.'

'Well, she scares the hell out of me,' Charles admitted. 'About Hob. He's doing almost everything else but I still can't get him to sit at a distance.'

'He's young,' I reminded Charles, 'and young dogs can only learn so much at a time. When they develop a blind spot, you just have to go slow and not imprint the wrong messages. Work on something else and come back to it after a few weeks. Sooner or later the penny will drop and you'll wonder what you were worrying about.'

Charles looked down at . . . Hob, and I saw his face soften. I would have to remind him to be firm. Spaniels are masters of the art of getting out of hand.

'You've got a deal,' Charles said. 'But, if it wouldn't hurt your feelings, I think I'll take him away until this is all cleared up. Otherwise . . .'

'You'd be waiting for it to happen again,' I finished for him. 'I'd probably be doing the same.'

I hurried Charles back to the house and got a cheque from him before he had a chance to change his mind, although I considered that unlikely. A bond was developing before my eyes. A satisfying part of my life was as a marriage broker between man and dog, promoting attachments which often lasted longer and gave more satisfaction than the master's other marriage.

The day was being frittered away. Dusk was almost on us again. Beth was in the garden again, sanding the paths in the failing light, with Sam in his private enclosure nearby. I had the kitchen to myself for once. This time when I tried the number I got an answer in a female voice.

'Mrs Campsie?' I asked.

'She isn't here at the moment and I don't have time to talk.' She sounded harassed. It was a young voice, presumably the daughter's—June, that was the name. 'Unless

. . . Where are you calling from?'

'Roughly, between you and the road bridge. I'm John Cunningham, at Three Oaks Kennels.'

'Oh, I've heard of you. And you want Mother? Listen, I'm in a jam. Mother's train comes in to Cupar in about fifteen minutes and I'm supposed to meet her but the car won't start. I think it needs a new flint or whiffletrees or something. I've been phoning round trying to get a garageman or a taxi or anybody, but every number's engaged or they've all gone to the moon or somewhere.'

'Would you like me to fetch her?' I asked.

'Would you? Please? You could collect me on the way if you like, but I'm all filthy from trying to get the horrible, beastly car to start. Honestly, it belongs in the South Ken. Science Museum. And the dogs are all over the garden. By the time I'd be ready she could have walked here.'

'Don't worry about it,' I said. 'I'll be quicker going straight there and I'll need my time. You'll get her back safe and sound in about half an hour.'

'Thanks.' I could hear the relief in her voice. 'You're a pal.'

I disconnected. She had not, it seemed, been brainwashed by her mother and Mrs Garnet into thinking of me as the root of all evil. It occurred to me to send Joe in the hope that he would ingratiate himself, but he was in his

155

workaday clothes. Even if I had lent him our car in the stead of his old van he would not have impressed a potential mother-in-law.

I favoured Beth with a very brief explanation and took off in the car. Dark was fast approaching. On the way I began to wonder how I would recognize Mrs Campsie. I had only the vaguest recollection of the banner-waving zealot in tattered waxproofs at Lord Crail's gates. The local worthy coming off the train was unlikely to present the same picture. But I need not have worried. When I reached Cupar Station, the train had called and left and a solid figure in blue, complete with hat and gloves as described by Joe plus an unsuitably short skirt, was pacing to and fro in the lamplight forecourt.

She glanced at my car in hope but then lost interest. I pulled up beside her and got out. 'Mrs Campsie?' I said. 'My name's John. June asked me to pick you up. She's having trouble with the car.' When she hesitated I added, 'You can always phone her for confirmation, if you think I may be a kidnapper.'

She looked at me sharply and then laughed a surprisingly musical laugh. She barely came up to my chin. She had a round, bland face with a large mole which had the look of a beauty spot although I was prepared to bet that she had to trim the hairs from it daily. She had on rather too much of a floral perfume which would have suited a younger woman. 'If you were daft enough to kidnap me instead of June I doubt if you'd be clever enough to hold me for very long. My suitcase is over here.'

I fetched her case and heaved it into the back of the car, thinking that if she had a heavy suitcase with her she must have been away from home for too long to have been our culprit. Of course, her daughter might have carried on the war . . . But, according to Joe, the daughter paid only lip service to her mother's views.

'John and June,' Mrs Campsie said musingly as she settled herself in the passenger seat clutching a large handbag. 'Have you known June for long?' Evidently her daughter's men-friends were more significant than any risk of being kidnapped.

I got in and restarted the engine. 'Neither long nor well,' I said. 'I just happened to be available when she was desperate for a car to go and collect you. Have you had a good journey?' The Campsie residence was not far from Cupar. The sooner we got onto the subjects I wanted to discuss the better, but I needed an opening.

'Very satisfactory,' she said. 'Killing two birds with one stone.' She seemed quite unaware of how inappropriate the metaphor was on the lips of an avowed animal rights activist.

'How's that?' I asked, politely but trying not

to show any excessive interest.

'I've been visiting my sister in Chelsea. But I did manage to join in a march, protesting at the export of British calves for veal.'

'Good for you!' I said. 'I'd be happy to see it stopped.' I was quite sincere. On the whole, I feel that well-meaning fanatics get very uptight over perfectly ethical activities or minor abuses which fade into insignificance when seen in the context of the terrors of nature. In the wild, it's a rare creature that is privileged to die peacefully of old age. Predation, disease, starvation and cold are the killers. But I have never come to terms with veal. I accept it if a hostess puts it on my plate but I would neither order it in a restaurant nor let Beth serve it at home. I regret this, because the meat is so delicious; but the price in animal distress is too high.

'Oh, I am so glad you agree. Can you pull over for a minute?'

She was surely not going to try to seduce me on the back seat as a gesture of solidarity. Just in case, I stopped under the brightest street lamp.

Her intent was not amorous. She rooted in her handbag and came up with a page from a Sunday paper. The headline referred to the protest march and a large photograph showed some of the leaders with Mrs Campsie, as she proudly pointed out, prominent in the foreground.

I congratulated her and drove off. We left the lights of Cupar behind. There could no longer be any suggestion that Mrs Campsie had been in our vicinity on the previous day and probably not for several days before that.

Apparently she had not exhausted the subject of her concern. 'And then there's battery chickens,' she said. 'Have you any idea of how cruelly they're kept and transported and killed?'

I said that I had. I forbore from pointing out that I probably had a much better idea of it than she had. I had noticed severed feet beneath the wire cages on a transporting vehicle.

'And the ones that they say are free range are mostly nothing of the sort,' she said indignantly.

An idea had fumbled its way into my mind and I started speaking before I had really thought it out. 'I never eat supermarket chicken,' I said truthfully. 'No taste and too much contamination. My friends and I have solved that problem, at least to our own satisfaction.'

Until that moment I had been no more than an audience and a possible suitor for an unmarried daughter, but now her awareness of me sharpened. 'Have you?' she asked quickly. 'How's that?'

'We go in for really and truly free-range poultry. We release the birds onto farm land from six or seven weeks old. We still provide feed but we hope that they're supplementing it with insects and seeds. If necessary, we pay the farmer to plant suitable strips of feed and cover. Four or five months later, when they're fully grown, we start to recover them for the table, but if we get only fifty per cent of them back we think it worthwhile. With a little luck, some of the others may breed in the wild. Doing it that way, there are no additives, no salmonella, no avoidable suffering. They're truly free range.'

She must have been tired from her journey because she still had not caught on that I was talking about pheasants. 'That sounds wonderful,' she said.

We were arriving at what I thought was her gate, which stood wide. The front door was open, spilling light and dogs. I had to speak quickly. 'What's more, we take a pride in trying to make death, when it comes, as merciful as possible. We try to make sure that they go out on a high point and never know what hit them.'

I got out of the car and hoisted her case out of the back. She thanked me absently. 'How do you manage that?' she asked.

I dropped back into the driver's seat. I had to speak up to be heard above the welcome that the dogs were giving her. 'With a shotgun,' I said.

As I drove off, I glanced in the mirror. A slim figure had come out of the house and joined her mother but the older woman was rooted to the spot, looking after the departing car.

I did not suppose that I had made an instant convert. If the next time that she carried a placard protesting against Lord Crail's shoot she wondered for a moment if she might not be making an ass of herself, I would be satisfied. But of course I was unlikely ever to know. On the whole, I thought it improbable. She was of a type which was easily inflamed but not given to rethinking established attitudes, or admitting to any change of mind that took place. All the same, I was glad that I had spoken out. I despise people who would turn us into a nation of couch potatoes or channel us into activities which they, and only they, consider to be politically correct. It will be a poor world when we no longer sail the oceans or dive under them, race on horseback, jump out of aeroplanes, box and wrestle and, of course, pursue our own meat.

As I neared my own front gates, my mind was taken up with my own form of bigotry, so that when my headlights caught a scruffy figure idling along the verge and kicking an empty can against the high stone wall of the garden I nearly ignored it. But I had no difficulty recognizing the lanky form and translucent hair of Tom Shotto.

I stopped a few yards short so that my lights would illuminate him and got out of the car.

161

Seen close to he was even less prepossessing, being moist as well as spotty. He was dressed in his usual jeans, which were tattered in a way not prescribed by any designer, and a worn leather jacket with suspiciously bulging pockets. A brand-new pair of trainers made the rest of him look even more tatty by comparison.

'What the hell are you doing here?' I demanded. I was angry. Disreputable and hostile teenagers were not to be welcomed. I would have laid hands on him if he had not been such a sorry specimen. Deep down I was afraid that he would burst and spray me with something dreadful.

'You've no right—' he began. His voice turned into a whine. 'It's a public road.'

'My garden isn't a public park for glue-sniffers,' I told him. 'Have you been giving yourself a buzz on the other side of the wall?'

He seemed about to deny it but then to decide that lying would be too much effort. 'I thought of it,' he admitted. 'But I was jumped on by a big, rough-looking bastard.'

'And kicked out of there? Serve you bloody well right,' I said. 'I've warned you often enough.'

'I never came near here again for weeks,' he said. 'It's getting more difficult to find anywhere. I was using a phone-box but they took it away.'

'You were daft to start coming back here at

all. Didn't the police tell you that we'd had a dog poisoned.'

'That was nothing to do wi' me,' he said shrilly. 'Why would I? The snoots believed me.'

His voice reminded me of something. After a few moments the penny dropped. 'Who put you up to making a threatening phone call?' I asked him.

'I didn't.' His look of outraged innocence could have passed for genuine. 'I bloody didn't. Never.'

Something else clicked together in my mind. 'That phone-box. The one you were using for your trips. Was it at Stouriden?'

'Not far. Why? What's it to you?'

'Then that was your shoe-sole stuck to the floor? When did that happen?' He shrugged helplessly. The days of the week meant very little to him. 'How many days ago?' I asked.

'Three. Two, maybe. Or four. See, I'd bought a tube of superglue—'

'Shoplifted it, more likely,' I put in.

He did not pause to deny it. 'I thought superglue would give a superbuzz. Losh, I was wrong about that! But it was enough that I dropped the tube and trod on it without noticing. A whole big tube,' he said plaintively. 'A while later I found that my shoe was stuck to the floor. And could I get it off without ruining a good pair of trainers? Could I hell!'

'An expensive evening for you,' I said.

'Yeah.'

163

'Getting back to that phone call—'

He was just the type to have been bribed to make the phone call while the real culprit established an alibi elsewhere—a plan which would have been damaged severely when the message was left on our answering machine and remained unnoticed for an indeterminate period. I was about to pursue the matter but his nerve suddenly broke. He ducked past me, grabbed up an old bicycle which I had not seen lying among the dead weeds and cranked his way towards the village.

I could easily have overtaken him in the car, but what then? The more pressure I put on him the less sure I would be of the truth of his answers. Let him sweat for a day or two, I thought, and then approach him through one or two of his contemporaries with a mixture of threats and bribes and we would turn him inside out. Tom Shotto was not the type to keep a secret for long.

The chill of the night was beginning to eat into me. Counting on the shelter of the car, I had hurried out without a coat. I got back into the warm and drove the short distance to the house. The glow of lights through the curtains made the old farmhouse look infinitely welcoming. Dinnertime had come and gone, but Beth had saved my portion in a warm oven. While I thawed out and ate and she attended to a sleepy Sam, I gave her the details of my outing.

'Our list of suspects seems to have been cut down to two,' she said at the end. 'One who we only know has a gruff voice and one we know nothing about at all. If you're right and that was Tom Shotto's voice on the phone—and I'm not saying that you are, the voice could have been almost anybody's—he's our best link. Leave it with me. I'll have a word with Daffy in the morning.'

'You think she—?'

'It's possible. Or if she can't, Rex almost certainly can. He talks the language.'

I had to agree. Despite his current yuppie image Daffy's husband had once been a real tearaway.

'Or there's Guffy,' I suggested.

Beth thought it over while absently stuffing Sam into his pyjamas. 'No,' she said at last. 'Too dangerous—for him, I mean. The boy doesn't have all his marbles. He'd make a better suspect than an investigator if there was any sign of him among Ben Garnet's clientele. Poor Guffy couldn't be trusted to keep a secret and we'd be setting him to ask questions about somebody who isn't averse to bonking people with heavy objects.'

'I suppose you're right. Failing which,' I said, 'Mrs Garnet may still come up with something.'

And so she did, but it was not in the least what we had been hoping for.

I gave the Garnets' answering machine a call but there was nothing new on it except for a message from a man who I recognized as one of Dundee's shiftier councillors, enquiring, rather anxiously I thought, after Ben Garnet's prognosis. I listened carefully in the hope of detecting some hint that the councillor's anxiety was for a promised puppy, but matters canine were not mentioned. Even from the guarded words it was clear that some devious and probably illegal deal was in the offing.

Mrs Garnet phoned an hour later and it was at once clear that this was no longer the same vaguely affable woman. 'How could you, Mr Cunningham?' she squawked indignantly. 'You deceived me, and you a captain!' She was sounding like a betrayed virgin but I could not find an opening to say so. She also seemed to think that a captaincy was a guarantee of veracity which I knew from experience to be far from the truth. 'You assured me that you were just about to sign the Kennel Club form but Ben says that you're still shilly-dillying or whatever the proper word is and that you were pulling my wool in the hope of getting me to tell you things and I think that that's despicable.' She paused to draw breath.

'I don't think that I told you anything of the sort,' I said quickly. 'I said that I wanted to speak to you about the purchasers of the pups, which was perfectly true.'

She set off again at a gallop. 'You said you wanted to know who they were so that you could be sure that they were going to good

166

homes, and I respected you for that, fool that I was, but Ben says that you only wanted to know who they were so that you could approach them and tell them that Ben's puppies are unpedigreed and sell them your puppies instead and leave him stuck with the whole of Cleo's litter. I don't think I ever heard of anything so dishonest. You lied to me!' she finished furiously.

Although I might have been guilty of tampering slightly with the facts, this diatribe was a bit rich coming from the wife of a man to whom it was almost an article of religion never under any circumstances to tell anybody the truth if a lie would serve the same purpose. But there was no point in saying so or of prolonging our talk. I hung up on her and decided to go for a stroll around the kennels. First I put on a warm coat. My body might as well stay warm while my spirit cooled off.

It very soon cooled right off. Whichever way we turned we seemed to be finding another blank wall. If we had had the powers and resources of the police we could have kicked the walls down and progressed. But as it was, we did not, and we would have to make do with what we did have.

The dogs had been fed and settled and were paying no attention to Joe and Dave, who were taking their guard duties seriously and patrolling around the paths between the runs while arguing amicably about the troubles of the world, the relative merits of certain ladies of their acquaintance and the best way to pluck a pheasant. I reminded them again that every word might be overheard in the house.

'We caught a peelie-wallie loon ettling to sneak in,' Dave told me. 'We kicked his arse and told him to go home to his mummy. Was that wrong?'

'Quite wrong,' I said. 'You should have drowned him in a bucket.'

CHAPTER EIGHT

There came another morning, Monday, the start of another week. Our competition commitments were coming ever closer and still we had made little progress towards identifying the threat which was hiding so tantalizingly remote and yet had struck down poor Accer. If the same threat had also struck down Ben Garnet, well, too bad! He could look after himself or at least he could try. In the past, he had proved remarkably adept at looking after what he no doubt regarded as Number One. Poor Accer had not been given the chance.

Daffy arrived early with her husband in tow. The two of them totalled little more than my age between them but they always gave the impression of being years ahead of me in worldly wisdom. When I first knew him, Rex had been just another long-haired yobbo, but a job on the oil rigs and the money that went with it had not turned his head. Marriage and Daffy's hard common sense had seen to that. Instead, Rex was now a respectable citizen who usually dressed as if for one of the better golf courses although that day he had dug out some of his cast-off gear as being more suitable for the day's errand. That Daffy still decked herself out as if for a pop concert or the Chelsea Arts Ball was a great disappointment to him but he lived in hope of coaxing her into the proverbial little black dress or a twinset and pearls, given time.

Secretly, I hoped that he would fail. I welcomed a touch of colour and eccentricity in my otherwise conventional life. Daffy was certainly not extravagant with it. She had the knack of taking an old tablecloth or pair of curtains, borrowing Beth's sewing machine and within five minutes looking fit for an appearance on *The Clothes Show*. That day, she was arrayed in what could have been mistaken for Victorian underwear except that it was in a fabric which I recognized as being from a bedspread seen in a recent village jumble sale and, I thought, she looked good. Some day, I was sure, this talent would be discovered and we would lose her to television or the rag trade.

With Rex briefed and sent off to see what he could get out of Tom Shotto, I had time to cogitate. It seemed to me doubtful that Rex still had a common wavelength with the young and feckless Shotto. Anyway, the more pressure that could be put on Tom Shotto from different sources, the sooner he might crack and reveal who had put him up to making the phone call—if, indeed, my guess was good and it had been his voice on the recording. I had seen young Guffy in his company at some time in the past.

Keepers usually make as early a start as kennel-owners, so I phoned ex-RSM Fergusson. He was at home and breakfasting—after doing the rounds of his snares, I was given to understand. I asked for Guffy.

'Yon laddie!' Fergusson snorted indulgently. 'He's no' here yet and the day half gone. What was it about?'

I had decided, for better or worse, not to shout this particular business from the rooftops. 'I have some work that needs doing—digging particularly.' This much was true.

'Wi' a machine? He's handy that way but he's no' insured for them.'

'By hand, with a spade,' I said. 'There's no access for a machine to where I want the work done.'

'Ah. He's a strong back, right enough.'

'I thought that he might like to earn some extra money in his own time. Would you mind?'

'No' in the least. Have him any time you like, for a' the use he is around here the noo. He might be glad of the chance to earn some siller towards the pup he's so set on. Nothing but the

170

best for yon loon.'

His words put a thought into my head, perhaps because to my mind any pups from our bloodline were the best. 'He wouldn't have his eye on one of Ben Garnet's pups, would he?' I asked, half joking.

'I wouldn't think it. He was wi' me when Mr Garnet came in-by to ask would the laddie do some gardening work for him. Guffy asked him about a pup and Mr Garnet said they was all spoken for and anyway the price would be away beyond his pootch. Shall I have him phone you when he comes in?'

'Please,' I said. 'But don't raise his hopes. Make it clear that I'm still not prepared to sell him a pup.'

'I understand, though he could be trusted no' to bad-use it—I'd see to that.'

'I'm sure. Please, just tell him to come and talk to me as soon as he's knocked off and had his tea.'

'That I will,' said Fergusson.

The routine of the kennels was already rolling. For lack of anything else useful to do about our current problem, I gave the two cockers a good workout with the dummy-launcher and then did my share of exercising the boarders. Joe was at work and when Dave expressed a wish to go down to the pub for an hour or two I said that I would stand guard in his place, which I did with the dart-gun near at hand, while monitoring Sam in his enclosure and at the same time teaching several young dogs the elements of retrieving with tennis balls on the lawn.

That took care of the morning and, on the principle that if you are doing three things at the same time you may as well do four, gave me time for some more thinking; but by early afternoon I was no further forward.

It was as a last resort that I sat Sam down on the kitchen floor with his building blocks and tried the Garnets' number again. I came up on the answering machine. I started the cassette recorder and sent the signal. The machine started to replay messages.

And I found that I had struck oil at last.

The man with the gruff and gravelly voice had made another call. The message was longer this time and I was sure that the accent was American or Canadian. 'Jamie here again,' he said. 'For God's sake get your finger out. I've got to know about that pup right away or I'll lose the chance of the other one. Call me back today and tell me that the pedigree for your one is guaranteed or I'll take the one that Steedman has for sale. I'm only holding off for the moment because I'd rather have a bitch. I'll be waiting for your call, but not for long. Goodbye.'

'Bloody hell!' I said aloud. I looked up Paul Steedman's number in my diary. Like us, Paul bred and trained springers. In theory he was a business rival but, although we gave no quarter when we found ourselves opposed in field trials, in fact we got on well and derived some benefit from helping each other out in times of trouble.

I heard his phone ringing in distant Blairgowrie. Paul's wife answered—a plain woman with a beautiful voice which, over the phone, was positively arousing. A few moments later Paul came to the phone.

'Tell me something,' I said after the opening greetings and a polite exchange of news. 'Who's the man with the scratchy voice who's dickering with you for a pup? Jamie something.'

'James Kirkmichael?' Paul sounded amused. 'If you're aiming to steal another client off me, steal that one. He's been dithering for so long that I sold the pup he was after. Mine was only his second choice. I was going to ask you for a near-enough match if he ever came back to me.'

The cloud which had been hanging over me began to let a little sunshine through. 'But do you have an address for him?' I asked.

'Just a moment.' I heard paper rustling. 'He lives in Glenrothes. No, I don't have an address. You want his phone number?'

He read the number out to me and I wrote it down.

I was looking up the name in the directory when Beth came into the kitchen. Sam looked up and smiled his most endearing smile.

'Bloody hell!' he said in what was a fairly close simulation of my voice.

For a moment, Beth refused to believe her ears. Then she looked from me to Sam and back again. It was clear what was in her mind. I was teaching her son bad language. If there was any cussing to be done, she would do it. To me. Later.

'You'd better listen to this,' I said hurriedly. I played her the section of tape on which I had recorded both the message and my call to Paul Steedman. 'And,' I added, 'his address is in the phone-book.'

'Wow! Berl...' There was a long pause before she went on. Sam and I waited anxiously. '... looming good!' Beth finished.

*   *   *

If I phoned a complete stranger to ask him where he was when my dog was poisoned, he would have more chance of getting cooperation from the police than I had. A visit to Glenrothes was called for. And then something clever. Just what, I had no idea. But clever it would have to be.

I set off straight away with Beth's admonition to be careful still in my ears but not in my mind. She always told me to be careful and I thought that I always was. The short day of the Scottish midwinter was already far advanced and a low sun flickered in my eyes as

I drove.

Less than half an hour brought me to Glenrothes.

Britain's new towns may be monuments to governmental penny-pinching. The aphorism about ships and ha'porths of tar might well have been coined about them. But at least they were designed around contemporary forms of transport instead of having evolved haphazardly out of the era of the horse and cart. A free-flowing traffic system brought me to where I wanted to go and—something which would never have happened in an older town— there was vacant and free parking almost on the doorstep.

Mr Kirkmichael's address was in a long three-storey row of flats. I walked up one flight. Peering in the dim light I found his name on a door and rang the bell. On the drive, I had decided that I only needed to know where he had been on the Saturday afternoon. I had concocted a story about a car being damaged in a car park and another car seen nearby that was thought to be his, which I thought would surely provoke an innocent man into telling the truth. A dog-poisoner might even confess to the vehicle damage, thinking it a cheap price to pay for a valuable defence of alibi.

My mental effort was wasted. The door opened, silhouetting a large figure against the equally dim light of a small hallway. Before I could open my mouth, he said a rude word and

175

swung a punch at me, aiming for my jaw. I ducked but not in time to avoid the punch altogether. It caught me over the right eye. I went down, more from surprise than either pain or the impact.

My wits were scattered by the unexpectedness of the attack. Before I could gather them, I heard another exclamation in a very different tone of voice and I found myself lifted and half carried into the flat, through the hallway and into a well-lit sitting room where a television was muttering in a corner.

At first, I could only think that I was being kidnapped, to be freed only on signature of the Kennel Club form. Then I made out what my attacker was saying. It was the voice that I had purloined from the Garnets' answering machine, like a match being struck on an empty oil drum.

'I'm sorry,' he said, lowering me into a soft leather chair. 'I'm real sorry. Could you use a Scotch?' The accent, now that I heard it without the distortion of the phone, was definitely American rather than Canadian.

I said faintly that I could. With water, no ice.

'Right away.' While I nursed my eye I heard him pouring. There was no blood but already I could feel the start of the swelling.

He put a tumbler into my hand. It was a very good malt whisky, which somehow finally dispelled the idea that he might be a kidnapper. 'Hang on,' he said. 'Let me get you

176

a steak for that, or something close.' While he was out of the room I took a one-eyed and slightly blurred look around. The room was meticulously if not imaginatively colour coordinated. The furnishings had been expensive but were showing the first signs of wear. A room that was comfortable rather than smart. A child's sweater was airing on the radiator and there was a sewing basket beside my chair.

He came back and handed me what turned out to be a lump of liver, very cold on a paper towel, and sat down opposite me. 'Gee, I'm sorry,' he said. 'I took you for somebody else, somebody I was good and mad at at the time. I still am, come to think of it. You sure look like him. But I'm real sorry. I should've made sure it really was the right guy on the mat. Then I should've smacked him hard enough to rattle his grandchildren.'

I held the liver against my right eye, which was rapidly closing all the same; but my left had stopped watering and I managed a look at him. He was about my height but at least twice my weight. I thought that he was in his fifties but be seemed very fit and even more strong. It seemed that he would have been more than capable of the attack on my *bête noire*, although he would not have needed to use a weapon— his fists looked more than adequate. His nose had been broken at some time and badly set, but in other respects his strong eyebrow ridges,

177

high cheekbones and full mouth reminded me very much of a corporal who had served with me. I find that people who look alike usually have other characteristics in common; and Jenkins had been a good-hearted man with a temper that could flare on the instant but cool as quickly. I decided that I was probably safe from further attack.

'You're talking about Ben Garnet?' I suggested.

Anger stirred again for a second but he only said, 'That cunning, conniving, devious bastard!'

'You've summed him up,' I said. 'You do know that he's in hospital? You didn't put him there?'

He looked at me in surprise and then laughed. 'Hell, no. It's news to me. Good news. If I'd had the pleasure of putting him in dock, why would I have taken you for him?'

'You could have thought that he was out and about again.'

He nodded, reasonably. 'Well, I didn't. When did it happen?'

'Four nights ago.'

'When I put him in hospital, as I surely will, believe me, he won't be out in four days. And I only flew back into this country Saturday night.'

'You're in the oil industry?' It seemed a reasonable assumption.

He nodded. 'I'm a directional driller—the guy who flies out to tell the engineers what to

178

do to get the drill-string back on track and doesn't get believed until they try it.'

'What's your quarrel with Ben Garnet?' I asked.

He frowned, but his usual amiable expression returned in a few seconds. 'You ask a hell of a lot of questions for a guy who hasn't even told me his name. But I guess I owe you an answer or two.

'I get to retire in a year's time. I'll be sticking around in Scotland—my father's family came from hereabouts, my wife's a head teacher here and I've a daughter in college and another still at school. When they put me out to grass, I reckon to do some hunting—this is good country for geese and I'm in what they call a shoot the other side of Kinross. I'm fixing to buy a house so's I'll be able to keep a dog the way it should be kept and I want to start a pup soon so's it'll be ready when I am. Even now, I'm often at home for weeks at a time; and if I had to go back to Africa or Oman I could put the pup to a pro for training. There's a guy called Cunningham near here that I've heard of. I phoned him once, spoke to his wife I guess, but at that time he didn't have any bitches coming along. Maybe I'll try him again.'

Isobel's certainty that she had heard the voice was explained.

'So I want a pup,' he resumed. 'I want to get fixed up now before I get sent offshore again. And I surely like your English springers. I'd prefer a bitch so's I can get a pup to follow on if she turns out good and I'd like to try my hand at working tests and maybe even field trials if we're good enough. I wasn't going to take a mutt that was bred in the back yard by some guy looking to make a few bucks—I shan't have the chance to start over again at my time of life. There's never a guarantee of surefire success, but I want the nearest I can get. Who doesn't?

'A breeder called Steedman had a pup spare but it was a dog. Somebody put me in touch with Garnet, who had a litter. He isn't a professional breeder but he showed me the two pedigrees and there were more champions on them than you could shake a stick at—field-trial champions, not show dogs. Well, to cut a long story sideways, he was convincing and against my better judgement I got talked into the back-yard deal. I picked out a bitch pup I surely liked. He was charging an arm and a leg, but OK, the breeding was better than just good. Then there was some problem over the pedigree and an unregistered pup wouldn't be a damn bit of good to me. Garnet kept promising and promising that it'd come out right but I wanted it in writing and he kept slipping out from under.

'When I got back this time, there was still no word. Today, I went out for an hour and when I came back just now there was a message on my answering machine from Garnet's wife, saying that the pup wasn't available after all,

180

he'd decided to keep it for himself. Not a word of apology. So I phoned Steedman but he said he'd had to let the pup go. I called Garnet's number again and only got his machine and I left a message calling him every name I could think of. That was just minutes before you showed up. When I opened the door and saw just another tall, thin streak—you don't mind?' he asked anxiously.

'Not if it's true,' I said.

'Yeah. It jumped into my mind that he'd come to pick a fight over my message. And I remembered that he'd been keeping me on a string and now I wouldn't have time to get a pup and turn it into a trained worker before they put me out to grass and I just boiled over. I'm sorry.'

'It's all right,' I assured him. 'Somebody put Garnet in hospital, mistaking him for me, so I suppose it was my turn.'

Kirkmichael, I was sure by now, was not the guilty one. I told him the story. It took some time and several more drinks and by the time I left, with an order for one of Dahlia's pups subject to satisfactory introduction, I had a new friend. I also had a load on board—if I had had the use of both eyes I would have been seeing double. Kirkmichael wanted to drive me home, but he had absorbed at least as much as I had and then, if we arrived safely at Three Oaks, somebody would have had to turn out and return the favour.

181

So I refused the kind offer. In retrospect, I think that I am glad that I did so; but sometimes I wonder what I would have done if Kirkmichael had been driving.

I drove myself home, very carefully but not so meticulously as to attract attention. I went by a back road where I knew that the police very seldom lurked. I felt good, and it was not just the effect of a very good malt whisky. If I was disappointed that we were again running short of suspects, I was pleased that we were getting facts.

I think that I was smiling as I turned in at the gates and somebody tried to kill me.

CHAPTER NINE

Later, it was explained that if the shot had been fired a moment sooner or later I would have been dead. And if I had braked at once he would have been able to have another crack at me.

I knew nothing of that at the time. My mind was far away when I heard a hell of a bang and felt a myriad tiny hammer-blows to my face. And then the shock became pain and the pain was becoming agony and I seemed to be unable to see. I meant to tread on the brakes but I hit the accelerator instead. For once, my automatic pilot failed and the car surged up the drive and onto the lawn before some long standing habit pattern took over and guided my foot to the brake.

Then there were people around me. Joe and Dave were shouting to each other. I recognized Beth's voice, high and quick but fighting to stay calm, and a part of my mind reached out to her for rising high above panic. But I was confused and disoriented, my world was upside-down and I took refuge in the one question that is always asked—'Where am I?'

'You're in the middle of the lawn,' Beth said. For some reason, that seemed to satisfy me. 'You stink of whisky,' she added.

'So would you,' I replied. God alone knows what I meant.

They were putting cloths over my face and wrapping bandages around, which did little for the pain but made it easier to keep my eyes still and closed. The effort of not distressing Beth with anguished noises was enough. And then an ambulance came. I recognized the sounds. Somebody stuck a needle in my arm and in moments I was away with the fairies.

That was pretty much the story of the next twelve hours or so. For seconds at a time I was aware of riding in the ambulance, of being wheeled from place to place and back again. I woke up once to find my bandages being changed under a dim light by a fluorescent green nurse. She explained that the colour had been put into my eyes to show up damage and foreign bodies. She was promising me that the colour would go away when I drifted off again.

I was vaguely aware of being unwrapped and examined several more times, of being stuck with needles and of being told to keep still for X-rays although I had already made up my mind never to move again. In between times, I was in another world and groping in black velvet for half-forgotten dreams.

I surfaced for a few moments in the morning. A voice that reeked of officialdom was asking for a statement, but I had little to say and what I did try to articulate came out as a garbled mumbling that even I could make no sense of.

Then they wanted me for surgery and I was plunged into the deepest sleep yet.

When I awoke, it seemed to be no more than a moment later. My face was more comfortably bandaged and although there was still pain it was more orderly and I knew that it would go away in time. My mind was clear again. I was more concerned about my eyesight than about discomfort but none of the passing voices could tell me anything. One, that I guessed belonged to the ward sister, assured me that the consultant surgeon would be coming to see me. From the scarcity of the noises around me I gathered that I was in a private sideward. Nobody had asked me whether I wanted such privacy so I guessed that it was down to Beth and the firm's insurance package.

An early visitor was Inspector Burrard. He was in a less disbelieving mood than ever before. I could see his line of reasoning. I would certainly not have exposed myself to such pain and danger in order merely to distract attention from my own misdeeds. Therefore the threatening message was probably genuine. Therefore the poisoning of Accer might be genuine. Therefore there was a possibility that Ben Garnet had been whacked over the head by one of his many other friends and admirers. The Inspector was therefore looking for a double assailant and attempted murderer. He listened in silence as I went over our earlier information again and then brought him up to date.

He seemed slightly cheered that his case was now undoubtedly attempted murder, with resources to be allocated accordingly. He told me more than I was able to tell him. I had survived, paradoxically, because the shotgun had been fired at me from close range. A pattern of shot sweeps a path through the air which has been described as trumpet-shaped—remaining compact at first and belling outwards as it gets further from the muzzle. The shot had still been in a dense ball when it struck the car and, by happy chance, it had been centred on the windscreen pillar. The fringes of the pattern had managed to smash both the windscreen and the driver's window but in doing so had largely been deflected.

I had been very lucky. Lucky to be alive, that is. About my eyesight I was still . . . in the dark. The real meaning of that phrase was coming home to me.

The surgeon arrived, displacing the Inspector. His voice was assured and reassuring. He had recovered several flattened pellets from over my eyebrow ridge and fragments of glass from in and around my eyes. He thought that he had got it all, although he said that the green stain revealed everything but glass. It was, he admitted, too early to predict the outcome. The fluid in my left eye was still too clouded with blood for him to examine the retina. I was certainly in for a pair of handsome black eyes, he said. The tiny scratches to the cornea of my left eye might or might not dim my vision permanently, he thought probably not; but Kirkmichael had done me a favour by ensuring that my right eye was already closed.

I was roused from a light doze by the patter of small feet, the pressure of a soft body leaning over me and a shower of lightweight kisses on the unbandaged parts of my face.

'Again?' I said, taking a firm grip. 'Which of the nurses are you?'

'Pig!' Beth said. I could feel her shaking but without being able to tell whether she was laughing, crying or trembling with nerves. She pulled back, leaving a trace of tears on my chin, and I heard her pull a chair while still keeping tight hold of my hand. 'I've seen the doctor. He says you're going to be all right.'

'Which is good news when you remember that I wasn't exactly all right before.'

My attempt at humour fell flat. 'How can you joke about it? Somebody tried to kill you.'

'It isn't the first time,' I pointed out. 'Somebody was trying to kill me when they took a blunt instrument to Ben Garnet, but I'm still around. Did whoever shot me get caught? Inspector Burrard was here but he got kicked out before he could tell me anything.'

Beth's voice steadied. I could sense the effort. 'I'm afraid not. We were much too concerned about you.'

'And the lawn,' I said.

'The lawn was frozen too hard to take any damage. It's quite all right, you'll be glad to hear. Were you joking?' she asked sternly.

'Yes.'

'Well, it's not funny. We'd heard a shot and then the car charged across the lawn and stopped just short of ploughing into the house and you had blood all over . . .'

Her voice was rising again. I gripped her hand. 'It's all right,' I said. 'We're both here and all's well, more or less.'

'Yes.' She puffed out a gusty breath. 'Well, anyway, Dave did take a look along the road and Joe ran round the house but there was nobody to be seen in the darkness. We never heard a car drive off but by the time the police

187

arrived whoever it was had had pots of time to run off through the fields. Some CID men came and they tried to find footprints, but what with our footprints being frozen into the ground and then the thaw starting soon afterwards—it's raining now, did you know?—they didn't really have a chance.'

'I didn't really think they would,' I said. 'I eliminated James Kirkmichael, by the way. He was out of the country until Saturday night. He played me back a message on his answering machine from Mrs Garnet to say that her husband had decided not to sell him the pup after all. I think I've sold him one of Dahlia's litter.'

'That's all very well,' Beth said. 'But he didn't know that he wasn't going to get a Garnet pup and you've only his word for it that he was out of the country—'

'His wife came in before I left. She confirmed it.'

'Well, she would, wouldn't she?' (I thought that Beth had a low opinion of other women, or else she was judging them in the light of the fact that she would have lied her head off for me.) 'Or she may have been ... did her voice sound anything like the threatening phone calls?'

'Not a damn bit,' I told her. 'She's a headmistress with a deep voice and a rather ponderous way of speaking. And if we start inventing accomplices we'll have to start again at the top of the list. We may have to do that anyway. We only have one suspect left and we don't know who the hell he is.'

'I'd rather be down to one than be left with half a dozen,' Beth said thoughtfully. 'Don't you worry about it. Concentrate on getting back on your feet and don't even hurry over that. I'll have a good think.'

I relaxed. Beth may look like a teenager and too pretty to have more than three brain cells to communicate with each other, but in fact when she 'has a good think' she thinks to good purpose.

'You realize that I shan't be fit for Saturday?' I asked.

'I know. We'll just have to cancel the cocker stake.'

'Not a bit of it,' I said. 'Get Daffy and Rex to escort Isobel to the championships. Henry and Hannah can look after the place, guarded by Joe and Dave if they're still willing. And you take the cockers on.'

'And who looks after Sam, may I ask?'

'All of them. I'll do it if I'm at home, which I intend to be.'

Beth started to protest, but the prices commanded by our dogs were largely governed by the successes of their immediate ancestors in competition. I rode over her protestations. 'You've handled them often enough in training and you've been competing, quite successfully, with the personal Labrador that I tried to tell

189

you not to have. It's time you pulled your weight on the firm's behalf in trials.'

'You expect me to go and win—?'

'No,' I said.

'You don't?'

'Not unless luck's really running your way. I do expect you to get a place. Or a certificate of merit at the very least. Try yourself out if you can get home before dark—'

'It's dark now.'

'Is it? I can't tell the time and I don't particularly want to. Tomorrow morning then. Get Henry to shoot for you.' I thought about the cockers and where Beth, who was more used to the springers and to one very patient Labrador, might go wrong. 'Don't stand any nonsense,' I said, 'but don't work them for too long on barren ground. If they do what you tell them but with a "Can't you see I'm busy?" expression, knock off. Come back and tell me how you got on.'

'I suppose I'll have to try.' Beth sounded very put upon and yet stimulated by the new challenge. 'I'll be back to see you this evening if I can borrow Henry's car again.'

I was satisfied. Beth is far better at handling spaniels than she thinks she is and the cockers adored her. 'Phone our insurers about the car in the morning,' I added.

'It's funny how you always manage to be unavailable when the difficult things have to be done,' she said unfairly. 'Like filling up claim

190

forms. What do I put this time? "Shot to bits by dissatisfied customer"? The garage think they can put it back together again or we might have got a new one off the insurance. Guffy turned up first thing this morning, by the way, anxious to earn some money towards a pup. Do you think that Guffy should be a suspect?'

'I wondered,' I said, 'but on the whole, no. We haven't heard a whisper about him being one of the clients.'

'Who'd know, except himself and Mr Garnet?'

'Mr Fergusson would surely have known. But when I sounded him out, he said that Guffy had asked Garnet and been turned down.'

'Oh well. It was worth a thought. Sam doesn't like him.'

'Guffy's several pups short of a litter,' I said, 'and a child would sense it without understanding.'

'That may be it. I wonder that they let him loose with farm machinery.'

'Anybody can learn simple tractor-driving. They don't let him near the big stuff, but I've seen quite young children in a tractor's driving seat at harvest time.'

'I told Guffy my guess was that you wanted him to dig away the hump behind the barn and fill in the hollow beyond the kennels. Was that right?'

'Absolutely.'

'Oh, good!' her voice said cheerfully. 'He's
191

coming up to see me in the morning but I'll try to get back to see you whenever visiting starts. Shall I bring you some fruit?'

'I'd probably poke it up my nose,' I said. 'Bring me my radio. The music on the hospital earphones seems to be chosen by a coloured teenager with feminist tendencies.'

'Don't be racist. And anti-feminist. And ageist.' She kissed me fondly and left.

My next visitor did not kiss me, fondly or otherwise. I was getting handier at feeding myself and had managed the evening meal without making quite so much of a mess, or so the nursing auxiliary assured me. The main benefit of a room to oneself was said to be the undisputed control of a television, but that facility was of little use to me. Even when I had mastered the use of the remote control, the bursts of unexplained laughter and sound effects were maddening. I was just wishing that somebody would come and talk to me when somebody came to talk to me.

'Hullo, old son,' said a voice. 'They told me that you were in here. How are you getting on?'

The voice was familiar but so friendly and sympathetic that it took me several seconds to identify it. Then I remembered Ben Garnet's singular ability to be 'Hail fellow well met' even, or especially, with the person whose metaphorical throat he was about to cut. I decided that a reply in kind might possibly get me the missing name.

'Uncomfortable, but I'm told that I'll see again. You're getting over your bump on the head?'

His face was invisible to me, but if he resented having the potentially murderous assault on his cranium referred to as a mere bump on the head, his voice showed no sign of it.

'Much better,' he assured me. 'My memory's coming back, a little at a time.'

'You don't happen to remember how you proposed to persuade me to sign your form?'

'What do you mean?' He sounded less affable.

'I understand you told your wife, just before the attack, that you were on your way to see me and get me to sign your Kennel Club form.'

'Did I say that?' He sounded amused. 'Perhaps I intended to rely on personal charm and the power of rhetoric. Everything that's happened since I came round after the attack is clear enough, and most of my life before that day. It's the events leading up to the attack on me that are still vague. They tell me that they could come back at any minute or in a year's time or not at all.'

I wondered why he was explaining in such detail a matter which he could expect to be supremely uninteresting to me. 'You'd better be careful,' I said.

'Believe me, I had that in mind.'

'Yes.' I was groping towards the subject that

193

I wanted to bring into the open but in such a way that I hoped that he would mention it first. A direct question might switch him straight into his 'What's in it for me?' mode. 'For all you know,' I said, 'you recognized your attacker and he may be aware of it. Of course, general opinion is that your attacker mistook you for me—which could make a lot of sense when you remember that somebody took a shot at me last night. On the other hand, he may have good reason for having another go at you.' *Like most of the rest of Scotland*, I nearly added.

'Is that what happened?' he asked sharply. 'Somebody shot you? My wife said that nobody seems to know much but she thought that you'd been involved in an accident.'

'Deliberate as hell,' I told him.

There was a silence. I would have given a lot to have seen his face. 'Why would somebody want to knock you off?' he asked. There was a faint emphasis on the 'you'. I thought that he was slightly miffed that I was stealing his thunder.

It was my turn to pause for thought. 'There was a threatening message on my answering machine,' I said.

'Saying what?'

I decided to open up. 'Saying that there would be awful consequences if I didn't sign the Kennel Club form so that all your pups could be registered. Haven't the police asked you whether you were somewhere behind it?'

'No, they haven't got around to that yet.'

'They will,' I said, 'when you get your memory back.'

There was another and even longer silence. I thought that he might have taken umbrage or even walked out on me, but he was only weighing up the information to decide where his best interests lay. 'Never thought of it,' he said at last. 'But you've reminded me. You never did get around to signing the form. I have it here,' I heard paper rustle.

'Who do you suppose are now in the front line of suspects?' I asked him.

His reply, as ever, was directed to looking after Number One. 'Not me,' he said. 'Like yourself, I was a victim. And I was in here when you were shot.'

There was also Mrs Garnet, it occurred to me. She had sounded quite angry enough to have taken a shot at me. 'The police will certainly want a list of your clients for the pups,' I said. 'Who are they, by the way?'

Perhaps I had tried too hard to sound casual. I could hear the smirk in his voice. 'You tried to winkle that out of my wife,' he said, 'and got nowhere. The police may be entitled to that information, if and when they care to ask for it. You definitely are not. When are you going to sign the form?'

The time for soft words had passed. 'Certainly not before you tell me what I want to know,' I said. 'I hear that you decided to keep one of the pups for yourself. Start from there.'

'That's what you've heard, is it?' He was openly laughing at me. Then his voice became stern. I had dangled a hint that I might sign the form although I had no intention of doing so; but even so small a concession as to give me his clients' names in order to obtain what he wanted without hassle would have been anathema to him. 'You listen to me, Cocky,' he snapped. His voice dipped for a moment, I think as he looked round to be sure that the door was closed. 'Like it or not, you're going to sign that form. You seemed to think that I was pulling a fast one over the parentage of those pups. But how about if I have proof that you've done the same thing? You're in the business. Who's going to be hurt most, you or me?'

'What the hell do you mean?' I demanded.

'I have a witness who'll swear that you palmed off pups that weren't sired by the champion you claimed they were.' *So there!* added his tone of voice.

I had to think for several seconds to recall what he was talking about and then I laughed aloud. Immediately, I could feel Garnet's indignation radiating like heat. 'You've been speaking to Alfred Ashdown,' I said. 'He's a nutcase. Because of an imagined resemblance to one stud dog rather than another, he accused me of claiming the wrong sire. We had all four dogs genetically fingerprinted and it proved beyond doubt that the breeding was

196

exactly as I said it was. He ended up paying for the DNA tests and all the lawyers' fees and you'll do the same if you try that one, and quite likely the cost of a libel action on top. Stuff your form.'

I thought that I had pulled his teeth but I was wrong.

'You'll sign that form,' he said, 'or my memory will come back with a vengeance. And who do you think I was looking at, the moment before I was clubbed?

'I'm getting home, probably first thing in the morning. So you sign that form and you sign it now. You said yourself that the police will be along to ask questions. If that form isn't signed, they'll get answers you won't like one damn bit.'

I felt a piece of paper being pushed under my hand. My brain was racing to try and find an answer but I could only think of one delaying tactic. 'I'm not signing anything I can't read,' I said. 'For all I know I could be signing away my house or my whole business.'

'That's reasonable,' he said. He sounded quite surprised that we should have even this small meeting of minds. 'All right, then. I can get my memory back any time in the next day or two. Your wife will be coming in to see you. She can read you the form and guide your hand. But if I don't get that form by, say, tomorrow night, you're going to have problems.'

I heard him get up. 'Tell me, little man,' he said, 'what do you want to be when you grow up?'

'Try to think of a new insult,' I said. 'You used that once before.'

As a Parthian shot it was feeble and he treated it as such. He only grunted and shuffled out in his slippers, leaving the form behind.

CHAPTER TEN

I fretted for half an hour, shuffling a few facts and many suppositions over and over in my head, hoping that a simple solution would pop up somewhere and that I would recognize it on its way past. But the more I thought about it the more hopeless it seemed.

When I felt the wave of depression about to break over my head I decided to phone and ask Beth to come soon, now, and bluster her way in, never mind visiting hours. I started asking for the telephone trolley but it must have been in constant use. I knew that my irritation must have become obvious when a nurse asked me whether I wanted an enema. I nearly accepted it just to relieve the boredom.

Beth turned up at last, bringing my radio and a comforting presence. Instead of borrowing Henry's car again she had persuaded or permitted Henry to drive her and the two arrived together. Pleased as I was to welcome Henry's wise old brains, his presence meant renewed talk about my health, my eyes and how long I would be out of commission.

After ten minutes or so I managed to drop the subject and drag the conversation by brute force round to Ben Garnet's visit, his attitude and his threat.

Beth was immediately up in arms. She spoke about scratching his eyes out, but if Ben Garnet had walked into my side-ward at that moment she would have been furious enough to try to castrate him with her teeth. 'You didn't sign his blasted form, did you?' she demanded.

'You made me promise not to,' I reminded her.

'Just in case you weaken, I'll take it.' I heard paper being folded and the snap of a handbag.

Henry tackled the subject with more logic and less passion. 'It still seems to me,' he said, 'that the only other way out of your quandary would be to identify the real culprit.'

'I've been flogging my brains, such as they are, to do just that,' I said, 'and I still can't see how we can get any further.'

Beth had cooled down a bit. 'Charles spoke to Mr Sowerby,' she said. 'He—Mr Sowerby—said that he was taking the pup whether it was registered or not, because he isn't interested in showing or breeding or competing, he just wants a jolly good working dog. I think he's done a deal with Ben Garnet, a sort of mutual back-scratching.'

'That fits in with what I know of him,' I said.

'And I've been running up our phone bill. I thought I might check up on Charles. We still had his London number, so I phoned his wife and asked for him. She said that he left London to fly up here on Friday, which is what he told us.'

'Did she sound natural?' Henry asked.

'She certainly didn't sound as though she was putting over a rehearsed tarradiddle. I believed her. And I've spoken again to Mr Fergusson and to Guffy's aunt and other people and I can't find anybody who'd heard anything about him trying to get a pup off Ben Garnet. I'm running out of ideas. What are you thinking?' she asked Henry.

'Let's think together,' Henry said. 'Something may come out of it. You have one purchaser of Ben Garnet's pups not yet identified. For his own reasons, Garnet was not divulging the name.'

'He had his reasons,' I said. 'Sheer bloody-mindedness.'

'But surely the police would get the names out of him?' Beth said.

'Perhaps,' I said. 'If they cared to. But would they tell us? And would he necessarily tell them the truth if they did ask him? It would be a first if he did.'

'We would find out the names of the purchasers eventually via the Kennel Club registrations,' Beth pointed out.

'A lot of damage might have been done by then,' said Henry, 'and it might be too late for serious investigation and the gathering of proof. And again, suppose that Garnet had already picked out the mystery client as the double assailant and dog-poisoner. Would you put blackmail beyond him?'

'I wouldn't put anything beyond that man,' Beth said.

'There you are. If he could screw money out of his client some other way, would he still feel honour bound to part with a pup? He might cancel the sale of the pup and bleed the other man dry, in which case you would never identify him from the Kennel Club registration.

'But we do know where six other pups are going. So far as we know, none of the purchasers is unbalanced enough to make threats and try to carry them out just to make sure of a registered pup; but there's no limit to the extraordinary ideas some people can get into their heads. On the face of it, each of those looks innocent, but as soon as you accept the possibility of accomplices, the list is wide open again.'

'That is what I have been lying here and thinking about,' I said. 'And I don't see any possibility that we could mount that sort of an investigation.'

'The police could,' said Beth.

'Eventually,' I said. 'I don't believe that

Garnet ever saw his attacker. But if he doesn't get that form signed by tomorrow night, he's going to tell the police that I whacked him. Once they get that idea stuck in their heads again, their chances of coming up with the culprits responsible for shooting me and poisoning Accer will almost vanish.'

'We might trigger the police into doing the investigation for us,' Beth said thoughtfully.

'How?' I demanded.

'By feeding them some evidence. It needn't be exactly kosher—'

I felt myself shudder. When she felt threatened, Beth was capable of contemplating and even enacting the damnedest scenarios. 'By which,' I said, 'you mean that it would be faked. Don't even think about it. One hint of you tampering with the evidence is all it would take to convince Burrard and his boys once and for all that we were guilty of everything from murder to illegal parking. Did Rex get anything out of Tom Shotto?'

'Nothing,' said Beth. 'He said that the little drip denied everything and he was inclined to believe him, no more than that.'

'You could still try Guffy on him,' I suggested. 'He's more in tune with Shotto; I caught Guffy in our barn in the company of the glue-sniffing brigade once—I told RSM Fergusson and he hit the roof. I think he's tried to keep Guffy out of bad company ever since. But at least they might have a common

202

language, so to speak. And if Guffy is the culprit he might give himself away.'

'How?' Beth asked.

'How would I know?' I asked rhetorically. 'He might do something silly, like trying to fabricate a story to pin it all on Shotto. Something like that.'

'Is that a crack at me,' Beth asked in a small voice, 'for suggesting that we might give the Detective Inspector a little push?'

'It wasn't meant to be,' I said.

'That's all right, then,' Beth said. 'Talking of Guffy, I meant to tell you. Not one single damn thing is working out for us. Guffy phoned. He sounded fed up. He doesn't want the work any more.'

'Either he's gone off the idea of a pup,' I said, 'which doesn't seem likely, or else he's saved enough for the one he's after. Never mind; whether he wants to do the work or not, you could still get hold of him and sick him onto Tom Shotto. Offer him an inducement.'

'Have you changed your mind about letting him have a pup?' Beth asked.

'That I have definitely not!' I said. 'I couldn't trust him not to be too heavy-handed once the novelty wore off. But I might find him a pup from an accidental mating, one that would otherwise be put down. In those circumstances, the pup would be better off with a slightly dotty master than dead. I could give young Guffy a damn good talking-to first. It's worth a try.'

'I'll ask RSM Fergusson to sound him out,' Beth said. 'But, John, even if we do identify the culprit, isn't there a danger that he'll only be charged with the shooting and dog-poisoning? You could still be accused of the attack on Mr Garnet?'

'It's a possibility,' Henry said. 'But once the police were pointed at the guilty party they'd be duty bound to investigate him and his friends. And there is always evidence somewhere, to be found if they look for it. A rash word overheard ... blood on a hammer ... contact traces ... these things do turn up.'

'They do,' Beth said, suddenly brisk. 'But sometimes they need a little help. John, we're going to have to love you and leave you. I may be back over the next day or two if I can get away, but the weekend's coming closer and there are things to be done if we're to do ourselves justice, so don't worry if you don't see ... hear me, I mean. Just, please, concentrate very hard on getting better and getting home.'

I said that I would do that very thing.

'Good. If I can't visit, one of the girls may come and deputize for me.'

'How far is she expected to deputize for you?' I asked curiously.

'Not very far,' Beth said sternly.

*　　　*　　　*

As the last effects of the cocktail of

anaesthetics and painkillers wore off, I felt the effects of the damage and of the subsequent surgery more and more. The hospital and I each passed a restless night. I heard the ward rouse itself from a light doze, struggled messily with breakfast and then, exhausted, was falling into a deeper sleep when the consultant made his rounds, complete with his tail of acolytes.

In the carefully dimmed room the bandages were removed. I was relieved to find that, although I felt as if my eyeballs had been sandpapered and, because of the swelling, neither of my eyes could be dragged more than half open, the fluorescent green haze had dissipated and I could see quite clearly the faces which were peering at me. They were not very handsome faces, in fact some of them were downright ugly, but the reassurance this clear vision gave me rendered them beautiful.

'You're doing well,' the consultant told me as the dressings were renewed. 'One more day behind the blindfold and we'll consider exposing you to the light of day.'

I was also allowed out of bed, but this was not as much of a blessing as it might have been. Despite my one quick look round the room while the bandages were off, I never did find my way around the unfamiliar layout without falling over things. The sole gain was that, though the chair in my room was not very comfortable, sitting vertically in it made a change from lying flat.

The monotony was only relieved by a blanket bath, given me by a pair of young and giggly nurses who were quite prepared for a little ribald flirtation, and a single visitor from the outside world. Hannah had been deputized by the others to bring me soft drinks and encouraging messages and to take back news of my progress. Beth, she said, was working with the cockers and getting on very well in between dashing about all over the place in a hired car and making phone calls. Exactly what Beth was up to, Hannah had no idea.

Either my eyes were recovering or I was getting used to the sandpapered feeling, and my mind must have been easier now that Beth was taking action, because I slept well that night. In the morning the usual hospital routine, in which I was washed and wiped and emptied and refilled with breakfast, kept boredom at bay at first. Later, boredom was dispelled altogether by another visit from Inspector Burrard. He arrived, for once, alone.

The Detective Inspector was much more conciliatory than ever before. He asked after my recovery and commiserated that I was still in a state of blackout. He chatted vaguely without ever quite saying anything, until I decided that if he wouldn't get down to business of his own accord I would have to do it for him. 'Are you satisfied now that I didn't shoot myself, poison a client's dog and knock a neighbour on the head?' I asked him.

'Not a fair question, sir,' he answered cautiously. It was the first time that he had ever called me 'sir'. 'And not the kind of question that I'm ever prepared to answer until a charge is laid. You may be free to jump to whatever conclusions you like, but I'm not. I'm still at the stage of asking questions. I can only tell you that I think the end is very near.'

'I'm relieved to hear it,' I said. 'Are you recording this?'

'Just to help my memory.'

'Go ahead and ask your questions.'

Instead, the Inspector went off at a tangent. 'That wife of yours,' he said. 'She's a very remarkable young woman.'

'No doubt about that,' I agreed.

'She seems so young . . .'

'She's twenty-nine,' I said. Even so, I was giving Beth the benefit of a year or two.

'Is she, by golly? That makes it a little easier to believe.'

'Makes what easier to believe, Inspector? That she's taken over the initiative? Hijacked your investigation?'

'She's been in touch with you, has she, sir?'

'No,' I said. 'But I know how she operates. She's done it before. You can trust her,' I added. 'She won't be trying to pull a fast one, nor to steal your thunder. Like you, she just wants the truth.'

'She seems certain that she's getting it. She may be right. But I wish I knew how.' The

Inspector sounded wistful. 'She sounds confident and she makes a certain amount of sense but she doesn't explain herself. How am I supposed . . .?' His voice tailed off.

It sounded as though Beth was beginning to get results. All the same, I was not in a mood to let the Inspector ramble vaguely. 'Since I don't have the faintest idea what you're talking about, Inspector, I can't help very much.'

'I think perhaps you can,' he said. 'Your good lady is adamant that the criminal in this case is obsessed with obtaining a puppy. A spaniel puppy. A working spaniel puppy,' he went on, 'of specific breeding, complete with authenticated pedigree. You know the field, Mr Cunningham. Does it make sense to you?'

'I'm afraid it does,' I told him. 'Dog fanciers, especially in this country, can get more obsessive than almost any other group of fanatics. If one of them is a few grams short of a litre and has developed a fixation, especially about breeding or competing—and the two go hand in hand, Inspector, because success in competition goes a long way towards selling pups—then you wouldn't believe how far he or she would go. At the top level, it has ceased to be sport and has become business, and cut-throat business at that. Chicanery doesn't happen very often, but I've known records to be falsified and once I saw a handler, who thought he was out of everybody's sight, sprinkle pepper on another competitor's dog.'

I heard a small sound as though the Inspector was scratching his head. He was certainly scratching something. 'Who can you think of,' he said at last, 'who would be capable of that sort of obsession?'

'I can think of one or two professionals or would-be pros who'd boil their grandmothers down for dogfood if they thought they could gain an advantage that way. Your problem may be that the average juror might not believe it— unless the procurator fiscal can get a jury of dog-lovers, of course. In which case they'll probably side with the accused.'

The Inspector was determined to persevere. 'But who can you think of around here?'

'That might be difficult,' I said. 'We've been taking a look at Ben Garnet's customers. The only fanatic we've found is Mrs Campsie. She's an anti-sporting fanatic, but whether she's fanatical about the dogs themselves I don't know. And the destination of one of Garnet's pups is unaccounted for.'

'I'm given to understand that Mr Garnet intends to keep two pups for breeding.'

That made me open my eyes even if they could only see a faint glow from beyond the dressings. I could do without an indiscriminate breeder producing litters of pups from our line almost on my doorstep. Every hard-won triumph in field trials on our part would go towards marketing his pups as well as ours. 'Did Ben Garnet tell you that?' I asked.

'When I last spoke to him he just smiled,' said the Inspector curtly. I could imagine that smile and it would have made the Inspector want to hit him. 'It was Mrs Cunningham who made that allegation.'

'Did she say where it came from?'

I heard the Inspector sigh. 'Like Mr Garnet, she just smiled.'

'A smile which made you want to turn her over and smack her bottom?' I suggested. 'No, don't answer, Inspector. You needn't incriminate yourself.' I was going to go on and say that I knew that smile only too well. When Beth produced it, she not only knew that she was right but she nearly always was so.

But at that moment I heard a repetitive noise which I put down as coming from some piece of hospital equipment until I overheard the Inspector answering his personal radio.

'We've found it, Mr Burrard,' said a tinny voice, very short on consonants. 'A ball-peen hammer in the tractor shed. There's been an attempt to clean it but we found faint traces of blood and one hair. It's gone off to the lab. Shall we pull him in? Over.'

'Any prints on the hammer? Over.'

'Not to the naked eye. There's not much hope but we'll try the superglue cabinet. Over.'

'Leave him for the moment,' said Inspector Burrard. 'For all we could prove to the contrary, anyone could have planted it. He won't be going anywhere. Over and out. You

210

heard that?' he asked.

I assumed that he was speaking to me. 'I heard,' I said. 'I couldn't help it.'

'Of course not. I was just going to take you into my confidence anyway. About what we were discussing just now. How does Augustus Mason fit the bill?'

'Who?' I said.

'The boy you know as Guffy.'

That at least told me which tractor shed the hammer had been found in. 'I hope that he isn't guilty,' I said slowly. 'I like young Guffy. We need more people with sunny natures like his. But I must admit that he fits. At one time, he was mad keen to get a dog, but I understood that Mr Garnet turned him down. He's certainly capable of getting passionate on that subject or almost any other. And he's . . . well, the circuits aren't quite complete. God knows how he'd react if he thought that somebody was doing him down.'

'According to Mrs Cunningham, he's the culprit. But she can't offer us any proof. If there aren't any prints on the hammer, and I'll be amazed if we find any, there's no evidence at all so far to back her up. Am I supposed to take action on the basis of unsupported allegations?'

Burrard was sounding so much more lost than any policeman that I had ever met before that I took pity on him. 'I can tell you this much, Inspector,' I said. 'Beth may not yet have the sort of evidence you'd need for a court of law, but she never acts out of prejudice and not often out of female intuition. She'll have something to go on.'

'Then why won't she tell me what?'

'If I knew, I'd tell you,' I said. 'It may be something that she isn't saying aloud for fear of being laughed at. It happened before. She was right all the time, but nobody believed her. When she gets the rest, she'll come to you.'

'But it's my job to get the rest,' the Inspector said, sounding more plaintive than ever. 'Can't you persuade her to give me what she's got? Tell her that she's more likely to be disbelieved and laughed at if she makes accusations without backing them up.'

'She's given you Guffy,' I said. 'Now that you know what you're looking for you should be able to find it—such as where he was at the relevant times. You can't expect Beth to do that for you.'

The Inspector grunted. 'That young man spends his spare time and half the night out and about on his bicycle. There's no knowing where he was. If he's to be believed, which is far from sure, he has little or no idea himself. So far, all that we've been able to find out from other enquiries is that Mrs Cunningham has already asked the same questions and got the same useless answers. But go on thinking aloud.'

'What you really mean,' I said, 'is that you're

giving me an opportunity to tell you what Beth knows, but I'm afraid that if she knows anything she's kept it hidden from me.'

'I never suggested such a thing,' the Inspector said with an indignation which I thought was feigned. In my little dark world I was becoming expert at reading hidden meanings in voices. 'You're an intelligent man and you probably have more information than I have. I'm not saying that you're holding anything back,' he added quickly when I opened my mouth to protest, 'although I can't say as much for Mrs Cunningham. But you've lived with it and seen all the details that don't come over in a statement. You know the people. You may be able to suggest something I've missed.'

He let me sit in silence for a minute but, faced with such a flattering request from a police officer, my mind, of course, went blank. I heard footsteps in the corridor, the voice of a nurse and then the jingle of a trolley.

Suddenly my mind slipped into gear. 'The gun,' I said. 'I'm told that Guffy was refused a shotgun certificate when his doctor refused to say that he was all there. As I said before, the poor boy's one pup short of a litter. So he doesn't own a gun. As I understand the law, he can quite legally borrow a gun for use when he's accompanied by the occupier of the land, or on an approved clay-pigeon ground, but neither of those conditions would apply while he was taking a shot at me. So where would he

213

have got a gun from?'

'We looked into that,' the Inspector said. 'We found that he has been in the habit of borrowing a gun from Mr Fergusson, his superior. According to Fergusson, the boy was only given the gun under strictly controlled conditions and had to return it to the gun-safe under his personal supervision the moment that shooting was over. It turned out that there was a spare set of keys and that Mason could have known where they were kept. But go on thinking. You're doing fine.'

'I take it that you didn't find the cartridge case?'

His laugh was what is usually described as hollow. 'To match the imprint with a firing pin? Nothing at the scene. There was a fertilizer bag half full of them at the farm and I'll be surprised if there aren't a score or more with Mason's fingerprints and the firing-pin imprint from Fergusson's gun. The pellets recovered from the scene were compatible with the commonest game cartridge represented there. Number seven, the experts tell me. You were lucky that he didn't use something heavier. If he had had a load of BB, you wouldn't have got off so comparatively lightly.'

'What's Mr Fergusson's attitude?' I asked. 'How he is taking it?'

'Defensively. He wants to protect the boy, so he's making no admissions. I'm damn sure that he knows more than he's telling us. I can only suspect that he feels vulnerable over the gun and doesn't *want* the boy to be guilty.'

'There's more to it than that,' I told him. 'I've heard it whispered that Guffy's Mr Fergusson's grandson on the wrong side of the blanket. There's a resemblance, if you catch them in the right postures.'

'That could be useful,' the Inspector said thoughtfully.

There was only one use to which the information could be put. 'In cross-examination of Mr Fergusson?' I suggested.

'You've got it.'

'You make me sorry that I mentioned it.'

He let my comment with all its implications go by. I heard him stir as if to get up and leave, but once I had begun to think about the question of evidence my mind had begun to buzz. 'What about voiceprints?' I asked.

I thought that the sharp sound which followed was the Inspector snapping his fingers. 'I knew I could count on you to get me going again,' he said with satisfaction. 'Young Mason gave us a sample of his voice in the process of telling us that he wouldn't give us a sample. At the first attempt, the lab couldn't make a good comparison because the tape I made from your answering machine was too degraded. I arranged for a technician with better equipment to go to you and make a better tape but it hasn't been done yet. I'd better make sure that he does it before a power cut wipes off the message.'

We batted the subject to and fro without getting anywhere. To be honest, I was spinning out the discussion for the sake of his company. He might not be the ideal visitor but he was all I had. I think that he knew how I felt, because he sat with me long after it had become obvious that there was nothing more of any usefulness to be said.

When at last he got up to go, he had one last word for me. 'Get Mrs Cunningham to tell me what she's got,' he said. 'Or to tell you so that you can tell me. I'm spending police time and resources on young Mason. Any time now, my super's going to ask me what I have to go on. And if I have to tell him that I only have an unsupported accusation from a lady who looks like a teenager, well, I don't know . . .'

'The shit will hit the fan?' I suggested.

'Worse than that,' he said gloomily. 'Much, much worse.'

CHAPTER ELEVEN

The consultant surgeon did his solemn round next morning, accompanied by his respectful tail of nurses, students and juniors. I was tenderly unwrapped, examined and used as a demonstration object. Despite the bruising which surrounded both my eyes, the discomfort had faded to a passing ache and a persistent itch which I was quite unable to scratch. However, I found that I could see more or less clearly, if only for short periods before my left eye began to smart and water.

The consultant seemed pleased with my progress and confident that there was no debris left inside, so everybody else relaxed and gave me patronizing smiles. Provided that I took it easy, the consultant said, I would make a complete recovery. He wanted to keep me for observation for another couple of days, but at that point I began to rebel. The ensuing argument wasted a lot of breath and precious time and seemed to shock the hangers-on.

The consultant must have been a true male chauvinist, one of a dying breed, because he only relented when I complained that my business had been left in the hands of four women—not mentioning that I could have trusted them to run it for years in my absence. I could go home, he said at last, if I promised to rest, to wear a patch over my left eye for at least a week and dark glasses outdoors after that whenever I felt discomfort, to seek medical help at the least adverse symptom and to attend his outpatient clinic whenever he felt like making an appointment for me. Fingers crossed under the bedclothes, I gave him my solemn word. I would have promised him my favourite brood bitch for a bedmate just to get out of there, back to my own bed and the

217

company of my dogs and partners.

Now that I was able to get round a little and to see in a rather cock-eyed manner, I could go in search of the telephone trolley, give the evil eye to the old lady who was monopolizing it until she hung up and call home. Hannah answered, sounding harassed. Henry and Rex had already left to escort Isobel to the Spaniel Championship. Beth, she thought, would be too busy to come for me but somebody would be over with clothes and transport whenever they could manage it. Hannah sounded amused about something. When I pressed her, she admitted that there had been an upset before Isobel and her companions got away, but she refused to go into any detail except to say that it was 'nothing for me to worry about', a sentiment which usually causes me to expect disaster.

It was afternoon before Joe arrived, scandalizing the hospital staff by appearing in his working clothes complete with safety boots. He had brought my clothes and my Reactolite sunglasses, so I forgave him for any harm that he might have done to my image. I got dressed, said a hasty farewell to the nurses and made my escape.

After all the anaesthetics and bedrest I found that I felt distinctly feeble. Joe carried my almost empty bag for me up the steps to where his van was waiting. I kept my eyes closed for most of the trip but not because of any complaint about Joe's driving.

When we were clear of the traffic I said, 'I met Mrs Campsie the other day.'

'What did you make of her?' Joe asked after a pause.

'I've met a dozen like her, well meaning but with their minds blinkered to new ideas. At a guess, she went to a third-rate school where she was fed a lot of facts and off-the-peg, preconceived opinions, but nobody ever taught her to think. So, instead, she goes by gut reaction. Would you like my advice? You don't have to have it if you don't want it,' I added quickly. During my army days, the younger men of my company had often come to me for 'advice to the lovelorn', but I knew that unsolicited advice was often resented.

There was a longer pause. 'Aye,' he said at last. 'You've put your finger on her so far.'

I turned my mind quickly away from the mental picture his words suggested. I had no desire to put my finger anywhere on Mrs Campsie. 'She's not the type to change her mind easily,' I said, 'But if you worked at it you could get there. She sees the image, not the person, and she's old-fashioned. So never let her see you again without a smart suit on, complete with collar and tie.'

'I don't even—'

'Then you'll have to buy one,' I said, 'if you want to win the girl. Hair neatly cut, fingernails clean, talk "pan loaf" and agree with everything she says. Never let her see this van again, borrow Dave's car instead and give it a polish.'

'You think that would do it?' Joe asked doubtfully.

'In a month, she'll be ready to marry you herself.'

I think that Joe winced. The van swerved slightly.

At Three Oaks, Beth was struggling on the lawn with the two cocker spaniels under the critical eye of Sam. She seemed happy to call a halt. 'You still look as though you lost a fight,' she said. 'And that eyepatch makes you look like a pirate. Are you seeing all right?'

'You have a smudge on your nose,' I told her.

'And with the other eye.'

'It's still sore, but it can see.'

That seemed to satisfy her. She scrubbed at her nose with a slightly grubby handkerchief and sent me indoors while she kennelled the cockers. She found me in the kitchen, sitting in one of the basket chairs and wondering how soon I could decently take to my bed.

She dropped onto the chair opposite with Sam on her knee. 'We'll have to call it off,' she said despairingly. 'I'm getting nowhere. Those little ber-beggers don't want to do a thing I tell them. I'm going to withdraw.' That Beth should nearly swear, and in Sam's presence, was a measure of how low her morale had sunk.

'No you are not going to withdraw,' I told

220

her. 'After watching you for all of fifteen seconds, I can tell you exactly what the problem is. You're too tense and you're too busy thinking about Guffy. You're not giving the dogs your full attention and they know it, so naturally they're playing you up. Cockers are worse than springers that way. Relax and concentrate on them, don't put up with any nonsense and they'll jump through hoops for you. They only want to please but you're not giving them the right signals.'

She brightened slightly. 'You think so?'

'I know it,' I said. 'Now tell me, what was the flap about before Isobel went off to the championships?'

'How did you know about that?' she asked indignantly.

'Hannah let it out but she wouldn't tell me what it was about.'

Beth sighed and then choked back a laugh. 'Isobel went for a last walk with Sylvan over the fields. Sylvan found a place where the farmer had been marking some sheep with a red dye and she rolled in it. And, of course, it wouldn't wash out.'

'It's specially made not to wash out,' I reminded her.

'Isobel didn't want to go to the championships with a liver and white and scarlet springer. But I told her that you'd hit the ceiling if she backed out.'

The picture of myself as an ogre to my

partners was not one that I wanted to dwell on. 'It may not be a bad thing. Dogs with white rumps seem on average to do best in trials and I think it's because they catch the judge's eye. What didn't you tell Inspector Burrard?' I asked. 'And why? What made you so sure that poor Guffy was to blame?'

Beth got up, dumped Sam on my knee and began to bustle about. She always speaks most confidently while she is busily doing something quite different. 'I thought it might be Guffy long before that,' she said. 'He seemed to fit very snugly. On top of everything else, he was earning money as fast as he could, to save up for a pup, and then suddenly he didn't need it any more. But I didn't want to point the finger at him without any evidence because it could look as though I had a prejudice against him for being a bit dottled. Or else it was somehow a soft option. Do you know what I mean?'

'I think I do,' I said. 'To pick on the mental underdog would be an easy way out.'

'That's just it,' she said. 'But then, after Ben Garnet dropped his bombshell, I knew that I had to do something. I came back here and sat down wondering how to be sure. And it came to me that you'd shown me one thing that was worth a try.'

'I had?'

'Don't look so flabbergasted. Of course you did. So I started calling round people's answering machines, those that have the same kind as ours, and listening to their messages. Some of them were really funny. I struck oil quite soon. But of course I couldn't tell the Inspector that I'd got what I'd got by tapping into other people's answering machines. I'm sure it's illegal or something.'

'I don't think it is. But where was the oil that you say you struck?'

'On the Garnets' machine again. You remember that I hurried away from the hospital before the end of visiting time, so that I'd be home before she was?'

'Who was it from and what did it say?' I asked patiently. 'Even better, play it to me.'

'I couldn't keep a recording because I didn't have your tape recorder. It's part of your radio, remember?'

I counted slowly up to ten. For somebody so clever, Beth can sometimes be as daft as a Labrador puppy. With those threats hanging over us, she could have reminded me that my radio had another task to perform. For that matter, a few pounds would have bought another radio or a cassette recorder. I waited until I could trust myself to speak calmly.

'Tell me what it said.'

'It was Guffy's voice and it said something like: "Mrs Garnet says you're going to keep two pups and breed them yourself. You're a wicked so-and-so to cheat me after all the work I did for you and you owe me nearly all the money for the puppy. You're a rotten swine. I'm glad I hit you last time even if it was the wrong person and next time I'll get you on purpose." So, you see, I knew it was Guffy but if I said *what* I knew I'd have to say *how* I knew.

'And now,' Beth continued, 'I'm going to give you something to eat after which you're going to bed whether you want to or not and no arguments.'

The programme was attractive but my conscience was pricking me. 'With the others away, Hannah will be needing help,' I said reluctantly.

'She's got help. She has Joe and Dave eating out of her hand.'

'Dog biscuits? No, never mind.' I felt a huge yawn coming. 'You'll get no argument from me,' I said.

'There you are,' Beth told Sam. 'That's how to do it. Why can't you be more like your dad?'

'And remember those words,' I told him. 'We may need to cast them up to her.'

Five minutes later she told Sam, 'I did not mean you to copy your dad in your eating habits. Eat up and don't be picky.'

I had enjoyed my portion of sole with a poached egg, partly because it made a change from hospital food but more because I could see it. Now, my appetite satisfied, I pushed the half-finished dish aside. 'I understand why you're tense,' I said. 'The sword of Damocles may fall shortly.'

She shook her head impatiently. 'If I'm tense

it's because I'm thinking about proving who did all the naughties. I don't want him walking around loose if he's going to take another shot at you. I wouldn't worry too much about swords and things,' Beth said. 'I think I've pulled Mr G's teeth for him.'

I let the mixed metaphor go by. 'How?'

Beth glanced at Sam but he was paying no attention. Even so, she chose her words carefully. 'I let him have his form back, but not in front of witnesses.'

'Hellfire Creek!' I said. 'I thought he was only to get it back over our dead bodies.'

'There was no need to be quite so drastic.' Beth's internal smile escaped and grew into a grin. 'I didn't sign it. It had a signature that looks a little like yours but it can easily be shown to be a forgery. Somebody more or less unconnected with us did it for me.'

'Who?'

She glanced at Sam again. 'Rex,' she mouthed.

I saw where she was heading but I could also see snags. 'But if it comes to a court case, there will be fingerprints.'

'We always have spare copies of Form One,' she said complacently. 'I took a clean one out of the middle. He took it away, wearing gloves, and retyped it on his aunt's portable. All you've got to do is wait until Mr G has registered the pups. Then it's your turn to make a threat. Both those pups instead of a stud fee or you'll have him prosecuted for fraud.'

I whistled. 'And that's not drastic? You play rough,' I said.

'No rougher than he's playing. Leave it as long as you can so that he pays for all the inoculations and things. Then, any time that he gets uppity in the future, you could threaten to make him tell all his clients that their registrations are invalid. 'That,' Beth said happily, 'will teach him to mess us around.'

I was still sitting quietly, struck dumb in admiration of her sheer ruthlessness, when the doorbell sounded. Beth was still coping with Sam so I went to the door.

The visitor was a technician from the police laboratory. He was a chubby, friendly man who seemed to be entirely focused on his high-tech activities. He had brought a load of electronic gadgets with him. I took him into the sitting room and showed him the Reply 120.

'I'll be glad to get it back into service,' I said. 'God knows how many messages we've missed.'

'I've been busy,' he said in both apology and explanation.

I watched as he knelt and hooked up to the telephone and then replayed the crucial message. He taped it and then began to fiddle with an oscilloscope and something that might have been a laptop computer but probably wasn't. He said that the background noise was some kind of machinery, possibly a road drill. If he could find the two frequencies—the pitch of the sound and the intervals of the pulses—he could try to filter out those wavelengths.

I heard somebody else come in. Beth must have handed Sam over to Hannah because, curious as ever, she had come to join us.

The technician fiddled and cursed under his breath, listened to his headphones and made faces for a few minutes. Then he sat back on his heels. 'I can try for a further improvement in the lab,' he said, 'but this is as good as I can get it here.'

When he played it again, the buzzing had almost disappeared and the voice was much clearer. 'That's Guffy,' we said together.

'I can tell Inspector Burrard that you identify the voice?'

'Beyond doubt,' I said.

'That's that, then. Voiceprints will be more solid proof, but courts always prefer witness evidence.' He switched our machine back into its answering mode and began to pack up his gear. 'You can have your answering facility back. What a week! Two colleagues off with flu and a mini-crimewave in Kirkcaldy and Burntisland. I'll tell you, I felt like sticking my head in the superglue cabinet for a quick buzz.'

Beth frowned. 'Somebody else said something like that,' she said. 'What is this superglue cabinet?'

'We were only joking. Superglue gives a very poor buzz, little more than you'd get from any other vapour that was oxygen deficient. Not like a real solvent at all.'

'But what is the cabinet?' Beth persisted.

The technician stood up and stretched. 'There's no secret about it,' he said. 'Not long ago somebody discovered, quite by accident, that latent fingerprints can be brought up on nearly all previously difficult surfaces if the object was put in a confined space with a dish of superglue. The prints come up bright silver. What's more, they're absolutely permanent. Even sandpaper will hardly shift them, unless you rub down into the underlying surface. Well, good day to you both.'

I saw him to the door and returned. Beth was staring into space, her expression so vacant that, seen side by side with Guffy, she would have looked the less intelligent of the two.

'But of course,' she said suddenly. 'That has to be it.'

'What has to be which?' I asked reasonably.

She snapped back and became aware of my presence. 'You go to bed,' she said. 'You're supposed to rest. And I've got a lot to do. Give me the keys to your gun cabinet.'

I detached the keys from my key-wallet and held them out. 'You're not going to shoot somebody?' I asked.

'You're being silly, of course,' she snorted.

'That's hardly an answer. Do you mean of course you are or of course you aren't?'

'I want to borrow your lamp,' she said patiently, 'that's all. The bright one you use with a rifle. Is the battery up?'

'It should be,' I said. 'I used it when that fox started raiding the rabbit pen and I charged it fully up afterwards.' I thought of asking what on earth she wanted with a very powerful lamp which was normally only used mounted above the telescopic sight of a rifle, but I recognized her mood as one in which she always considered pausing to explain things a waste of valuable time. 'Shall I put Sam to bed?' I asked.

'Could you? Can you see well enough to manage?'

'He can do most of it himself,' I reminded her. 'He only needs to be supervised and to be told a story.'

'All right then. You put him down. Don't tell him any stories you wouldn't have wanted me to hear. And after that you go off to bed. I'll see you when I see you.'

'Very probably,' I said.

*　　　*　　　*

Much later, I was aware of Beth coming to bed. Later still, minutes later as it seemed, it was daytime again and I was alone. I could hear the usual working noises downstairs and out on the gravel. Suddenly I was wide awake and hungry, my eyes opened reluctantly but with no more than an annoying twinge, and my curiosity was overpowering.

Beth, I thought, probably intended to sneak

off without me in order to spare me what she regarded as unnecessary stress. I washed sketchily, skipped shaving, dressed hastily in yesterday's clothes and, pausing only to pass a brush over my hair, hurried downstairs.

I found Beth in the kitchen and in the process of handing over responsibility for Sam to Hannah and Henry jointly. She already had her coat on. 'I'm going out in a minute,' she said to me.'

'Hold on,' I said. 'You're not leaving me behind.'

Beth looked hard at me. 'You look awful,' she said, 'but not as awful as yesterday. Take some cereal. There's still some toast and coffee. But get a wriggle on if you want to come. Inspector Burrard's coming to fetch me in about ten minutes. We're going to Freddy Crail's shoot, where it all began.'

'We could have driven there in fifteen,' I pointed out.

I was about to ask her what was going on, but she said, 'That gives me ten minutes with those blasted cockers,' and dashed outside.

I took as much breakfast as I could manage in the time. Most of it I ate standing at the window. Beth was getting on much better with the spaniels now that she was concentrating on them. I was putting on a coat when Inspector Burrard arrived in a marked Range Rover. Gribble—I never did discover his rank—was at the wheel with the quiet Sergeant McAndrew beside him. There was another man beside the Inspector in the back.

The day was dark, and damp as well as cold. I would have welcomed back the snow.

Inspector Burrard opened a door but remained seated. 'Come with us, Mrs Cunningham,' he said. 'You can guide us and explain as we go.'

'All right,' said Beth. 'John, you could follow in our car. It'll save the Inspector having to bring us back later.'

'Good idea,' Burrard said. 'Go with him, Minnity, and give us some room.'

The fourth man obediently got out and joined me. The Range Rover was already moving. I fell in behind but I stayed well back. I knew from experience that the spray being thrown up by the Range Rover would be laden with the rust-provoking salt which had been put down to clear the ice.

'Do you know anything about what's going on?' I asked Minnity.

'Damn all,' he said. 'I'm a frogman, if that's any help.'

The more I thought about it the more puzzling I found it. Police frogmen were associated in my mind with dead bodies, but nobody was missing. Correction, nobody connected with the case that we knew of. Of course, we had not yet met Charles's wife. And no one would have bothered to mention it to me if somebody had disappeared—Charles

231

himself or Mrs Campsie or Tom Shotto. Had Guffy been to his work? There might be others . . .

We rolled up to the farm buildings and detoured around them. We took a track which brought us eventually near to the small loch. This covered no more than two or three acres. Crail was in the habit of releasing a few rainbow trout in the spring and pursuing them, usually in vain, during the summer.

Beyond the loch, the ground began to rise into the small hills which gave the shoot its character. In almost any other conditions than the dank and overcast weather of that day the loch was a picturesque spot, though trees overhanging the water made casting difficult. Under that charcoal sky and with the bare branches dancing to a sodden wind, it looked only fit to contain corpses.

The convoy stopped about a hundred yards short of the water. Minnity, we discovered, was already wearing his wetsuit under light clothing. While he was fetching his other gear out of the back of the Range Rover, I joined Beth and the other three men. A track, passable but rarely used except by Crail himself, crossed an unused area of stony ground which was ragged with grass and dead weeds. Beth was pointing along the track.

'Even by lamplight,' she said, 'I could see tracks where the weeds had been crushed down.'

The Inspector squatted down. 'There's been a vehicle along here, right enough. Within about the past week, for what that's worth. It could have been a farm vehicle.'

'I expect it was,' Beth said, nodding as though the Inspector had said something clever.

Burrard was too proud to ask for explanations. 'I see,' he said doubtfully. 'Very well. Gribble, do your thing. You didn't walk along the track, Mrs Cunningham?'

'I cut across the stony ground,' Beth said.

'Then we'll do the same.'

Gribble, who was evidently more than a mere driver, fetched a video camera from the Range Rover. We left him recording the faint signs of a vehicle passing and began to stumble across the rough ground towards the water.

We were checked by the approach of a Land Rover, which pulled up behind the police vehicle. Mr Fergusson eased himself out and came towards us, hurrying as much as his arthritis would allow. In his perturbation, his aches and pains seemed to be almost forgotten. If he failed to recognize the officers, the police livery on the Range Rover would have reminded him.

'What the de'il's adae here?' he demanded. I saw him lick his dry lips and I thought that he had his own suspicions.

'That is what I am waiting to find out,' Burrard said. 'Do you know where your assistant is now? Augustus Mason?'

Mr Fergusson hesitated and then shook his head.

The Inspector looked hard at the old keeper but must have decided that he was telling the truth. 'I suppose you have a right to come with us,' Burrard said, 'but you're not to interfere. Is that understood?'

The keeper nodded. 'I understand,' he said.

We set off again. The delay had enabled Minnity, now hooded and with his tanks on his back, to catch up with us. He had kept on his shoes and was carrying his flippers.

'What are they about?' Mr Fergusson asked me in a troubled whisper. 'Is't the loon?'

'I think so.'

'What's come o'er him?'

Suddenly I understood. We had seen no signs of Guffy recently. If he it was who had tried to kill me and failed, his next step might well have been suicide. 'I don't know anything for sure,' I said unhappily. 'But I think you should prepare yourself. It's not going to be good.'

He produced a sigh which seemed to come right up from his leather boots. 'Aye,' he said.

Beth and the Inspector were standing where the track arrived at the water. The further side of the loch was still frozen, but here, near where the feeder stream entered, the water was open. 'There was only one place I could think of to look for it,' Beth said. 'So I came here last

234

night with a bright lamp and a pair of Polaroid glasses—they cut out reflections,' she added.

'I understand,' Burrard said.

'Oh. Well, anyway, I was sure that I could see it.' She pointed into the water. 'Just below where we're standing.'

'Minnity,' Burrard said, 'in you go.'

Involuntarily, Fergusson and I took a step back from the water. I noticed that he was looking very white.

The frogman placed his shoes neatly together, one sock in each, donned his flippers, climbed carefully down the bank and entered the water. He was only hidden for a few seconds before he surfaced again. He nodded to the Inspector. Fergusson swayed and I caught his arm.

'It's there all right,' Minnity said when he had removed his mouthpiece. 'If it's what you were expecting.'

'Who?' Fergusson asked huskily. 'Who is it?'

'It's not a who, it's a what,' Minnity said, pulling himself up onto the bank.

'Then what is it?' the Inspector demanded querulously.

'A telephone kiosk, all in one piece, complete with phone.'

The keeper made a noise like a deflating balloon and sat down suddenly on a stump.

CHAPTER TWELVE

Detective Inspector Burrard shook his head as if trying to deter an unwelcome insect. Then he made up his mind about something and hurried back to the Range Rover. I could see him speaking over the installed radio with emphatic gestures which would have been lost at the other end. I helped the keeper back to his feet and the rest of us ambled more slowly back towards the cars. We walked dumbly, silenced by anticlimax and, in most cases, puzzlement. Beth was nodding to herself but deep in thought.

The Inspector had finished and restored his microphone to its place by the time we reached him. He got out of the Range Rover and we formed a small ring, our breaths steaming in the low sun and cold, moist air. I had the advantage of partial knowledge and I had a hazy picture of the truth; but the others were not so favoured and the baby-faced Inspector, in particular, looked as though someone had stolen his rattle.

'Mrs Cunningham,' he said, 'is that what you were expecting?'

'Yes,' Beth said. 'I didn't want to say too much in case I was making an ass of myself. But it did seem rather obvious.'

'It is far from obvious to me. You'd better spell it out.' He nodded to his Sergeant, who produced the small tape recorder, set it to work and placed it carefully on the bonnet of the Range Rover.

'You didn't have all the facts,' Beth said kindly. 'I'll go back to the beginning. Somebody threatened us, attacked Mr Garnet in mistake for my husband and poisoned a dog.' As she spoke, Beth was avoiding Fergusson's eye. 'We're not concerned at this moment with who or why, what we're considering is the evidence you need and I think you have it now.

'On the day of the keeper's shoot, Guffy was sent to the phone and came back to say that the phone-box at Stouriden had vanished. John and I drove round that way before following Mr Fergusson back to our home and, sure enough, the phone-box had gone and there was the sole of a shoe stuck to what had been the floor. There was also a strip of new tarmac not far away, as though the road had been up not long before. That was two days after Mr Garnet was attacked and just before the dog was poisoned.

'John got hold of that boy Tom Shotto, the glue-sniffer who you caught hanging around our place. He said that he'd been in the habit of using that phone-box for his sniffing but he'd dropped a tube of superglue and trodden on it. Last night your technician mentioned that fingerprints shut up in the fumes of superglue come up silver and are absolutely permanent.

'What I think happened is this. Somebody used that phone-box to send us the threatening message. While he was speaking, some machine started up at the road-works nearby, but in his excitement he may not have noticed. Then, in order to ram the message home, he came to the roadway near our gate. Mr Garnet, who looks very like my husband in a poor light, was on his way to see John and he got in the way of a blow intended for John. It must have been a shock for the assailant, to realize that he had struck and possibly killed the man who he was trying to buy a pup from, partly by working for him in his spare time and partly by saving up what else he could earn.'

'Guffy?' Mr Fergusson said, his voice hardly more than a whisper. 'Guffy did a' that?'

'I'm afraid so.'

'I canna credit it. Och, ye maun be mislearit—'

'You promised not to interfere,' the Inspector reminded him. The old keeper, a man well used to discipline, was silenced.

'The fingerprints will tell you for certain who, among those who'd agreed to buy one of Mr Garnet's pups, had used the phone-box recently,' Beth said. 'To go on, it must have been another shock to remember that he had made the threatening phone call to our answering machine from that box. There had been roadworks nearby at the time and he thought that the recording of that sound would enable the source of the call to be pinpointed. So he went back to the phone box, intending to

238

polish away his fingerprints. In the meantime, however, Tom Shotto had trodden on his superglue and the fumes had then been confined for some hours in the little-used kiosk. Any fingerprints, including his own, were now bright silver and he found that no amount of polishing would remove them. If he was anxious before, he would be in a panic now. It must have seemed like a judgement on him.

'What was he going to do? The wisest thing would have been to do nothing. There must have been the fingerprints of dozens of people in that box and he could quite legitimately have made a call from there at any time. He chose the one course of action that might focus attention on the fingerprints. He came to the farm and borrowed the fork-lift and a spanner from the tractor shed. That would be easy enough. He's used to driving the farm machinery and nobody sleeps nearby. He unbolted the phone-box from its base, carried the whole thing back here and plopped it into the loch.'

Beth seemed to have finished. We digested her words. It all seemed quite obvious, now that somebody had pointed it out.

Mr Fergusson had always looked less than his real age, but now he might have been a well-preserved centenarian. He found his voice first. 'You're suggesting that my ... that young Augustus ...?'

The Detective Inspector might be ruthless in

239

pursuit of truth and the evidence to back it up, but I was to find that once a case had broken he was a compassionate man. 'A recovery vehicle is on the way,' he said gently, 'and a fingerprint expert. We had best wait to see what they find. Mrs Cunningham has found the evidence for us but she may have drawn the wrong conclusions.'

'Aye,' said the keeper glumly. 'Maybe.' There could be no doubt that he was already convinced.

As Beth neared the end of her explanation, I was distracted. Over the Inspector's shoulder I was watching as a stocky figure on a heavy old bicycle came down between the trees from the direction of Stouriden, bumping and juddering over the ruts and potholes in a track intended only for forestry vehicles. I half hoped that he would turn around and go.

I still had an irrational liking for Guffy. He had, it seemed, killed poor Accer and tried to kill me. Anyone else doing the same would have had my undying enmity. I would have waited a lifetime for the chance of revenge.

But Guffy somehow did not fall within the rules. I could make allowances for his passionate desire for a dog of his own—an emotion with which I could fully identify—and for his damaged intelligence. His nature was usually cheerful and affectionate, two characteristics only too rare among much higher IQs than his. He would have to be

240

placed under control, but I found that I had no wish to be present at an occasion which must inevitably be painful, not least for his putative grandfather.

But there was nowhere for him to go and he must have known it. He stopped for a minute at the trackside. I could see by the stiffening of his outline that he had made up his mind. Whether he intended to face the music or to try and bluff it out I did not know, and nor perhaps did Guffy, but it was going to be one or the other. He was not going to run. He came on again.

The movement had caught Mr Fergusson's eye. He stiffened. I thought that he was going to shout a warning, but he saw the impossibility of flight and he beckoned the boy. Guffy rode his bike slowly up to us and put his feet down.

'What's up?' he asked. His air of innocent curiosity was unconvincing. Seen close to, the pinkness of his face was split into blotches of red and white and the shaking of his hands produced a sympathetic jingle from the bell.

We had arrived at a supposition of Guffy's guilt by way of logic perhaps tainted with the intuition which I had assured the Inspector never figured in Beth's reasoning. Even if Guffy's fingerprints should turn up in the telephone box, they could have been left there innocently. Until I saw the guilt that Guffy was trying to hide, I could still have believed him innocent.

But Mr Fergusson *knew*. He had studied the

boy for years and grieved over his mental state. He had learned to read his moods and watched his comings and goings. Without pausing to reason it out, he was sure.

'Why?' he asked the boy gently.

'Why what?' The effort to be casual was itself a strain. Guffy did not have the talent to carry it off. His voice was throaty with tension and I could tell that his mouth was dry.

'Why did you get tore into Mr Garnet? Why shoot at Mr Cunningham here? God's sake, why poison a wee dog?'

Guffy moistened his lips. He glanced around our faces and decided against a last attempt at denial. All colour was gone from his face now but he raised his chin defiantly. 'I was sorry about the dog,' he said. 'There was no other way I could think of.' He paused and we all saw his face change. The sunny-natured youth vanished and in his place was a creature capable of journeying to the furthest edge of anger. I thought for a moment that there was a keener edge to the breeze that ruffled across the loch. 'The bugger!' he shouted. 'He promised me, Mr Garnet did! If I howkit—'

'Dug,' Mr Fergusson wailed. Even in the face of disaster, Guffy was not to let his upbringing slip.

'—if I dug him a flowerbed and levelled the ground for a lawn, he'd allow me two quid an hour against a pup. He bloody *promised*. And I worked my arse off for him.' Guffy's voice dropped. He was crying unashamedly now. 'And I had the pup chosen and damn near enough saved to make up the difference. Ah, but she's a bonny wee bitch and came to me herself and settled in my hands. We could've made a rare team, I swear we could! I was going to be so patient with her, bring her along slowly, let her learn at her own pace the way you said.' Guffy's voice broke.

The Inspector looked anxiously at Mr Fergusson, who stepped into the breach. I would have expected him to take the boy's side, but truth and honour were dear to the old man. He chose his next question with care. 'Had you chosen a name?' he asked gently.

It was the right question. Guffy sniffed but pulled himself together and the frown left his face for a moment. He wiped his cheeks with the back of his hand, replacing his tears with smudges of dirt. He swung his leg over and stood his bicycle carefully at the trackside. 'I meant to call her Pearl, she was so precious,' he said. The frown returned. 'Then'—he cast me a look of reproach—'*he* wouldn't sign the paper for registration. A pup would be no good to me if I couldn't enter it in trials like the best dog-men do, like him and her'—he looked from me to Beth—'and ... and ... I could've raised pups myself.'

Clearly, Guffy had had his dreams. I felt a huge pang of misery on his behalf. He had been aspiring to the lifestyle that I had made for

243

myself. Perhaps he had even hoped to model himself on me. Poor Guffy might even have been on the verge of the one activity, perhaps even the one living, that was open to him, only to have it snatched away by Ben Garnet. Perhaps, if I had recognized his ambitions, I might have let him work at the kennels and gain a grounding in the many facets of dogwork. Instead, I had been the first to dash his hopes—but at least I had not raised them first to the skies.

The Inspector had a question on his tongue but Mr Fergusson was successfully coaxing his protégé to produce the truth. Burrard waited.

'So you tried to scare Mr Cunningham into signing the paper?' the keeper asked.

'Aye.'

'Say yes, Guffy. But it was Mr Garnet you hit?'

'Aye. Yes, I mean.' Guffy fell silent again but the need to explain overrode discretion. 'I took him for Mr Cunningham in the gloaming. He turned just as I came up behind him and he moved and I hit him harder than I meant. I still thought it was Mr Cunningham and I thought I'd killed him.'

Mr Fergusson shook his head sadly. 'That was no' wise,' he said. 'But what's done is done. What came next? They're saying a phone-box is down in the water. Would yon be the ane frae Stouriden?' For the first time since I had known him, Mr Fergusson was slipping back into his native tongue in front of the boy.

Guffy was nodding violently. 'I thought of the message I'd put on Mr Cunningham's machine, trying to scare him into signing the paper. There'd been the sound of a road drill not far off. I thought they might trace the call to the box at Stouriden. I'd heard of fingerprints and that they can match them to whoever made them, so I went back that night to polish them away. I could see them clear in the light of the torch, thousands of them and nothing to say which were mine. That didn't matter a damn because I was ready to polish the whole box. But they wouldn't shift, not one of them.'

'You werena' thinking,' Mr Fergusson said. 'Why would it matter if your fingerprints were there? I've sent you to make calls from that box often enough.'

'I never thought of that,' Guffy said wonderingly, impressed by such razor-sharp reasoning. 'It just seemed that with them shining like that and not rubbing off whatever I did, that they were accusing me, sort of. You know what I mean? So I fetched a spanner and the fork-lift from the barn and dumped the whole jing-bang in the wee loch.'

I glanced at Mr Fergusson to see how he was taking these revelations. When I saw the tears on his cheeks, I looked away. The Inspector, I saw, was doing the same.

'You've done a' the wrang things,' Fergusson said sadly. 'You puir, daft laddie, I doubt they'll ever let you have a puppy now.'

At this prophecy, Guffy threw his head back and let out a howl like that of a soul in torment, which perhaps he was. The sound wrenched at something atavistic in me and I felt it as a physical relief when the noise faded to sobs and died away. There was a silence but for his laboured breathing. 'D'you mean it? Never?' he said at last.

Mr Fergusson nodded sombrely. 'You should hae come to me the minute you kenned he was swicking you.'

This reminder of his grievance brought Guffy back to the boil. 'You ... mannie!' he said after a defensive glance at his mentor. 'I cycled to his house late yesterday to finish the wee bit work—'

'Little bit of work,' Fergusson said. It was more a reflex than a correction.

'Aye, that. The little bit of work. And Mrs Garnet came out to me and said she was to tell me that her man had changed his mind, he would be keeping two of the pups to hissel and my Pearl was one of them, and I could go hang.' Guffy's voice broke. 'My wee Pearl!' he wailed. He lifted the front wheel of his bike and slammed it down so that it bounced and every one of the many loose components rattled. And then he regained some control of himself. He lifted his bicycle and stood it carefully beside the track again. 'When I asked for the money I was due for the work I'd done, she said her man

246

had told her I was paid up to date. The bugger!'

'Ye mauna' cry the mannie a bugger,' Fergusson said. 'It's no' polite. But that's a dashed dirty trick on a young lad. Fancy a man wi' his siller takkin' advantage of a puir loon that way. You were daft to trust a lang-nebbit man sic as yon. The bugger!' he finished.

'Aye. But I'm upsides wi' Mr Bloody Garnet,' Guffy said, proudly, calming down again. 'I just been over there and I think maybe I killed him this time. He still wouldna' pay me for the work nor let me hae the pup, so I upped wi' a shovel and cloured him a good yin.'

'Hit him a good one,' Fergusson said mechanically. 'Oh my God!' he added.

The policemen had been standing by, letting the old keeper carry out their interrogation for them, but Guffy's last statement goosed them into action. Guffy, protesting only at leaving his bicycle behind, was swept into the Range Rover and I saw the Inspector using his radio as Gribble struggled to turn the big vehicle in the confined space left between my car and Fergusson's Land Rover.

I jumped to my car. Beth was ahead of me. 'I'm coming too,' she said. 'Mrs Garnet may need somebody with her.'

The old keeper was heading for his Land Rover but I was sure that his part was done. It would only pain him more to see the rest of the drama played out. I checked the car beside him. 'You should stay here,' I told him. 'They'll

247

need you to direct the recovery vehicle. Otherwise they'll break down the bank. I'll see that you're kept informed.'

It was thin. Probably he saw through it but accepted the goodwill behind my reasoning. He nodded and turned back.

As we took off after the Range Rover I saw a black figure in the mirror. It was Minnity, still in his wet suit, standing forlornly by the trackside with his flippers in his hand. His other clothes, I presumed, were still in the Range Rover. He seemed to be waving but perhaps he was shaking his fist.

*   *   *

Less than five minutes brought us to Garnet's house—an old farmhouse now modernized into an upmarket residence set in a generous garden and, in my opinion, far too good for its owner. Several figures at work on Charles's new house looked round in surprise as we swept past the paddock where three horses grazed. I glimpsed Charles himself with Hob in an adjoining stubble field. The spaniel seemed to be playing him up but I decided that this was not the moment to stop and pontificate. We arrived in the Garnets' drive right on the heels of the Range Rover.

Beyond the house and hidden from the paddock, a figure lay on the sodden ground.

Mrs Garnet was crouched over her husband.

She had covered him with a coat and rolled another to support his head. We ran to her. She was scared almost out of her wits but she had sense enough to say that she had called for an ambulance.

'And so have I,' said the Inspector. 'One of them should be here within minutes. For the moment, let me help him.'

Burrard and Beth between them drew Mrs Garnet to her feet. When she saw me, her eyes blazed and she looked to the Inspector.

'You've arrested him?'

Burrard was down on his knees. He looked up. 'Mr Cunningham has been helping us all morning,' he said.

'Then who—'

Sergeant McAndrew had stayed in the Range Rover with the prisoner, but Guffy managed to poke his head out of a partially opened window. 'I learned him,' he shouted. 'he swicked me and I cloured him. He should have treated me right-like.' McAndrew pulled him back. There seemed to be a scuffle developing in the back of the vehicle.

'Come into the house,' Beth said. She led the older woman away from the scene.

Gribble must have been both intelligent and quick because he appeared from the house with a wet cloth and a bowl of ice cubes. He delivered his burden to the Inspector. 'I'll mind the radio,' he said.

'And help McAndrew,' the Inspector said,

249

'before somebody gets hurt.'

He wiped gently at Garnet's head. As a crust of earth left by the weapon was washed away I saw that Garnet's brow was swelling and that blood was running from a cut. The blood, I thought, was a good sign, if one wanted him to live.

The Inspector sat back on his heels. 'He's alive. I can't feel any sign of a fracture. I think he'll make it.'

I tried to look pleased. 'What will become of young Guffy?' I asked.

He looked up from the improvised ice-bag which he was holding on the wound. 'The boy? There's no denying that he's made at the very least one murderous attack. The best advocate in the world couldn't turn the shot fired at you into anything less than attempted murder. But in this liberal-minded age, who knows?' The Inspector gave vent to a surprisingly human sigh. 'I'm sorry for the old man,' he said. 'Don't quote me, but you can suggest to him, as your own opinion, that because the boy's been registered as mentally handicapped, he'll probably be detained under the Mental Health Act.'

'Where?'

'Depends where they have a bed for him. Liff Hospital would be my best guess.'

I hoped that he was right. Liff, in Dundee, would be within easy reach for Mr Fergusson to visit. I had been imagining Guffy many miles away and among strangers. 'He'll be allowed out?' I asked.

'Not the least doubt of it,' the Inspector said disgustedly. 'If they're not actually foaming at the mouth they're soon turned out for the community to care for them. The old chap may have him back on his hands before he knows he's gone. Och well, I suppose it's progress of a sort.'

There was a sound in the distance. The Inspector looked round. 'Ambulance,' he said. 'You hold this in place.'

I knelt down and held the cloth and its cold contents against the wound. If I was tempted to make his condition worse, perhaps by pushing pebbles up his nose (which would undoubtedly have been blamed on Guffy) I resisted temptation nobly. Beth, after all, had handed me all the weapon that I needed.

Garnet stirred and his eyes, although unfocused, were half open and settling on my face. 'What . . .?' he said. 'What . . .?'

I hoped that he was taking in my words or at least that his memory was registering them. 'Tell me, little man,' I said. 'What do you hope to be . . . *if* you grow up.'

AUTHOR'S NOTE

Part of this book was written in the light of a passing comment by a police officer who spoke at the preceding conference of the Crime Writers' Association.

Just after its completion, I bought a copy of *Murder Under the Microscope—The Story of Scotland Yard's Forensic Science Laboratory*, by Philip Paul, published by Macdonald, at a large bookstore. ('You see,' I heard one member of staff say to another, 'somebody *did* buy it!')

I was discomfited to read that the superglue cabinet has to be heated. Not to a very high temperature, I should add; but I hurry to reassure any reader who chances to step on a tube of superglue while making an obscene or threatening phone call that he or she need not fear that they are perpetuating their fingerprints—not, at least, unless they are gifted with exceptionally hot feet.